DEDICATION

For Mel Michelle.
Thanks for asking for another silverback.
And for everything else.

Son of Kong

(Sons of Beasts, Book 2)

T. S. JOYCE

Son of Kong

ISBN-13: 978-1976392665
ISBN-10: 1976392667
Copyright © 2017, T. S. Joyce
First electronic publication: September 2017

T. S. Joyce
www.tsjoyce.com

All Rights Are Reserved. No part of this book may be used or reproduced in any manner whatsoever without written permission, except in the case of brief quotations embodied in critical articles and reviews. The unauthorized reproduction or distribution of this copyrighted work is illegal. No part of this book may be scanned, uploaded or distributed via the Internet or any other means, electronic or print, without the author's permission.

NOTE FROM THE AUTHOR:

This book is a work of fiction. The names, characters, places, and incidents are products of the writer's imagination or have been used fictitiously and are not to be construed as real. Any resemblance to persons, living or dead, actual events, locale or organizations is entirely coincidental. The author does not have any control over and does not assume any responsibility for third-party websites or their content.

Published in the United States of America

First digital publication: July 2017
First print publication: July 2017

Editing: Corinne DeMaagd
Cover Photography: Wander Aguiar
Cover Model: Jonny James

ACKNOWLEDGMENTS

I couldn't write these books without some amazing people behind me. A huge thanks to Corinne DeMaagd, for helping me to polish my books, and for being an amazing and supportive friend. Looking back on our journey here, it makes me smile so big. You are an incredible teammate, C!

Thanks to Jonny James, the cover model for this book and couple of my others. Any time I get the chance to work with him, I take it because he has always been a good friend to me. Thank you to Wander Aguiar and his amazing team for this shot for the cover. You always get the perfect image for what I'm needing.

And last but never least, thank you, awesome reader. You have done more for me and my stories than I can even explain on this teeny page. You found my books, and ran with them, and every share, review, and comment makes release days so incredibly special to me.

1010 is magic and so are you.

ONE

Torren had messed up again.

He blew out a frustrated breath and rocked his head back against the shower tile. The steaming water burned his mangled knuckles and ran rivers of dark crimson down the drain between his ankles. He'd been sitting here for five minutes trying to calm his heart rate, but it wasn't working. Nothing did anymore.

That guy deserved the beating he got.
Fuck you, HavoK.

The public had just recently named his gorilla. Havoc for the crew his sister was in but with a K because he was the new Kong. Clever. It suited his gorilla just fine, so he'd been calling his animal that ever since the name had been splattered over the news like road kill after Covington burned.

Three huffed breaths, and a snarl blasted up his throat. His body tensed painfully as the silverback tried to take it again. He was sitting under the running water, heat turned up as high as it would go. Gritting his teeth against the burning of his muscles, Torren slammed his head back onto the tile three times and clenched his fists on his bent knees so hard, his blunt nails dug into his skin.

Vyr needed to put him down soon. His best friend, The Red Dragon, hated discussing it, but they couldn't avoid it forever. Torren was a monster, and as much as he pretended to be a normal shifter, he simply wasn't. He was the son of Kong. Marked with a big birthmark that covered most of his back. A birthmark that said he was supposed to be the silverback of the biggest family group. He was supposed to be the leading silverback in his shifter culture. And what had he done instead? Shunned his people because they were damn-near evil, and he wanted nothing to do with them.

Too bad his morals were killing him.

Too long with no family group under him, and now his fully mature silverback had hopped the crazy train and was riding it all the way down to Hell.

A knock sounded at the door.

"No," Torren said, but his voice wasn't human. It was too low and gritty.

Another knock banged on the door.

"I said fuck off, Vyr!"

The door swung open so hard it banked on the bathroom wall with a crash.

"Technically," Nox Fuller said, "you said 'no,' and then you said 'fuck off.' Also, I'm not Vyr. Clearly. He is hideous, and I am the finest specimen of a man—"

"Nox, I'm in the shower, and if you say another word, I'm going to beat the shit out of you."

"Been there, done that, got the scars," he sang. He opened the huge shower door and, fully clothed in jeans and a black and white plaid shirt, sat on the other side of the sprawling shower, facing Torren. "Might wanna cover your dick-imus minimus. I can see your balls."

Torren rolled his eyes closed and counted to three so he wouldn't Change and rip Ob-Nox-ious's throat out. And while he did that, he also clamped his legs together. "You know how you asked me to tell you when you were acting inappropriately?"

"So we can laugh together, best-friend-style?"

"No, to teach you basic social interactions and manners. That's what you said."

Nox's blond eyebrows shot up, and he ran his hands through his laid-down mohawk. "Hmmm, I don't remember that last part. I just like when you tell me I'm being bad so I can smile."

"This is one of those inappropriate times. You shouldn't be sitting in the shower with me."

"Nevada said I need to try harder to speak your language."

"I don't know what the fuck you're talking about," Torren groaned out. He was so exhausted he would give just about anything to have the power to snap his fingers and wish Nox away. He needed a week off from this idiot.

"You gotta gorilla problem."

"Thank you for stating the most obvious thing on the planet."

"Like…you don't even try to hide the monster in your eyes anymore. You haven't had brown eyes in three days. I've been watching."

"Congrats on being a stage-five stalker."

Nox smiled. "Thank you. Speaking of stalking, I followed you to the sawmill and watched you beat the shit out of those three boar shifters. You're gonna start attracting attention our crew doesn't need. Vyr is gonna burn your body, eat you, and puke you up, then yell at you and eat you again."

"Well, what Vyr doesn't know won't hurt me."

Nox rested his head back against the tile and narrowed his eyes, looked down his nose at Torren. "You need poontang."

Torren frowned. He never could keep up with Nox's train of thought. "What?"

"A mate." He gestured to Torren's healing knuckles, still bleeding a snaking stream of maroon onto the tile and into the drain. "You need steady sex."

"I need you to leave."

"And BJs."

"Seriously, get out."

"Nevada gives me head like three times a week, and I feel fine."

"You Change all the time and you fight me every day."

"So? I still feel fine."

Torren heaved a sigh that turned into a deep rumble in his chest. Talking to Nox was exhausting. "I don't need a mate. I just need to be left alone for a little while."

"Well, as your new best friend—"

"You're not my best friend. I can barely stand you."

"Well, last week you said you hated me seven times, and now you can barely stand me so that's best-friend improvement. Plus, when you find out what I've done for you, you are going to fall into friend love with me, and Nevada will be proud, and I'll get even more head."

"Nox! Go. *Away!*"

Nox pulled a piece of soggy paper out of his back pocket, leaned forward, and handed it to Torren. "You're welcome," he whispered like a weirdo.

God, he hated Nox.

Torren snatched it out of his hand and unfolded it, ripping the wet paper in two places with his roughness. The ink was smeared, but he could still read it.

Cinnamon. There was a phone number underneath. "Cinnamon sounds like a stripper name."

"A hot stripper name," Nox agreed, nodding once. "And she's agreed to bang you once a day for two hundred dollars a week. She even promised to let you call her your mate."

Torren pressed the heels of his hands against his closed eyes to alleviate the headache that was building there. His right eye began twitching. Nox had that effect on people. "Can you please let me finish my shower now?"

"If you say I'm your new best friend. And that Vyr sucks and is a dickhole and you hate him."

"I'm not going to say that."

"Fine, say that you *strongly dislike* him."

Torren wanted to sleep for three days. Maybe Nevada would knock him over the head with a frying pan. Or maybe he could convince Vyr to burn him and eat his ashes now. It would be quick and painless, unlike this conversation that was killing him little by little.

"Whenever you're ready," Ob-Nox-ious murmured, flicking two fingers at him.

Torren offered Nox a slow, exhausted blink. "If you don't get out, I'm going to tell Nevada how you pissed on that electric fence when you were twenty-five and electrocuted yourself, and then you'll get zero head because she'll realize how dumb you are."

Nox's eyes went wide. "I'll see you at

breakfast," he rushed out as he lurched up and scrambled out of the shower. "Cinnamon is waiting on your call. Give her tube socks. Girls dig that shit." The door slammed closed.

Torren stared at his half-healed knuckles. He couldn't stop fighting, couldn't stop Changing, couldn't stop the anger that was always roiling inside of him. He could feel it—he was dangerous now. Not to Vyr and not to Nox, who could defend themselves from his gorilla, but from any dominant male—shifter or human—who crossed his path.

And for a moment, he considered the dripping piece of scrap paper between his fingers. A stranger mate wouldn't soothe him, though. She would make him worse. Angry at the world, he ran his thumb over the paper and smeared the phone number to oblivion.

Nox might have meant well, but Torren knew exactly what he was. He'd known it for years. He, Torren, the Son of Kong and the destined leader of the gorilla shifters, had shunned his fate. And in doing so, he'd made himself into a lost cause.

TWO

Candace Sumner shouldn't be here.

Not just in this town, or in the job she worked, or in the crappy apartment she leased, or even in this half of the country. She shouldn't be in the parking lot of the Foxburg Public Library. She definitely shouldn't be thinking of Nox Fuller's suggestion that she bone a gorilla shifter once a day for money. And she absolutely shouldn't be thinking about stalking the shy, curvy, mouse of a personality who had stood timidly against the wall when Nox came into Jem's Exotic Dance Room last week. Nevada Foxburg had been fun to hunt, but she was too people-shy and probably wouldn't give up any answers. Candace was going to have to take this slow and easy with her.

And yet, here she was, about to really do this. Because why the hell not? Her life couldn't get any more pathetic, really, so why wouldn't she take a stab at something better? Plus, she'd researched the Son of Kong. Everyone had started calling him HavoK, but in her mind, he was Prince Kong. He was seven shades of sexy, dominant male, and she was sick of feeling unsafe in her life. Maybe they could be good for each other. Or be friends. With benefits. At least for a little while before she chased him away like she did with everyone else.

When she'd tried to find the man who made the offer, Nox Fuller turned out to be a ghost. Candace had only had Nevada's first name to go by, but she'd been able to track her down easily enough. It was a unique name, and Foxburg was a small town.

Her old Volvo began shaking hard, and she gripped the steering wheel with one hand and turned it off quickly with the other. It was on its last legs, but she couldn't afford a new one. She was drowning under Dad's medical bills. She couldn't even afford an oil change right now. She was in such a desperate situation, she didn't know what else to do. The debt collectors were getting out of control, and she was spiraling trying to keep up with the bills.

God, she'd fallen so far.

She expelled an explosive sigh and glared at the small, beige brick library. *You can do this.*

Candace shoved the last three cold french fries from the bottom of the Wendy's bag into her maw. This was breakfast, lunch, and dinner today. Ninety-nine cent fries, because that's all the food budget allowed until she made some cash on her shift tonight. She had to make a hundred and fifty bucks to make her overdue electric bill tomorrow or her lights were going to be shut off. Again. And no electricity in a Pennsylvania winter was miserable. She knew, because she'd spent half of last winter with just a propane-powered space heater at Dad's house. *Fuck. Don't think about that.*

Candace zipped up her jacket and shoved open

her door, then slipped and slid across the frozen parking lot to the front door of the library. There was nobody there that she could see except for the curvy brunette, Nevada, behind the counter. Candace stomped the snow off her boots and approached the golden-eyed beauty. Carl would flip out if a girl like Nevada Foxburg came into Jem's looking for a job. He told Candace at least twice a shift she was too skinny and her boobs were too small. Carl was a sweetheart of a boss.

Before Candice reached the counter, Nevada had dropped her gaze to a stack of bookmarks. "H-hi."

"Hey. You came into my club last week. I don't know if you remember me—"

"Oh, I super-remember you. You wrapped your legs around a pole…and…shook your…you know." Nevada's face went bright red before she blurted out, "It was my first time in a strip club and I only went because Nox said everyone should go to a club at least once and also because he was looking for a friend for Torren, and I didn't mean to see your nipple tassels." The woman looked completely mortified as she clapped her hand over her mouth and whispered through her fingers, "But I did."

Candace giggled. "Almost the entire male half of this town has seen my nipple tassels. It's okay."

"Right. Are you looking for book recommendations? Or…"

"Yes," Candace murmured out of curiosity. "Lay it on me. What books do you think I need?"

"Ummm…you probably make a lot of cash, and we have a good business section. Bookkeeping for Dummies?"

Candace's mouth flopped open.

"Sorry, that sounded bad. I just meant it could help you keep track of your earnings. For taxes? How about step-by-step dance books? Not that you need help with that. You dance really…erotically."

Candace pursed her lips so she wouldn't laugh. She should possibly be offended, but this girl was kind of funny.

"Romance? I just read one about a pirate that was kind of good. I'm going to stop talking now."

Her voice had tapered off into a soft whisper and her cheeks were bright red.

That's when Candace noticed the scars. Nevada's left cheek was uneven with deep, silver scarring she'd covered with make-up. Huh.

"I'm pretty terrible at book-keeping and taxes. I get audited almost every year," Candace admitted to make her feel better.

Nevada covered her cheeks with her hands as if trying to cool them, or perhaps hide the scars Candace was staring at. Nevada offered a slight smile. "I get the feeling you aren't actually here to check out books."

"That I am not. I don't read much. Unless you count gossip magazines while I wait in line at the grocery store."

"Those totally count." Nevada scrunched up her nose. "Is this about Nox's business proposal the other night?"

Candace nodded.

"Yeah, I'm really sorry about him. He comes up with ideas, but sometimes they're completely inappropriate. I try to stop him, but—"

"I think it's a great idea."

Nevada must have sucked her gum down her throat because she horked it onto the counter and went into a coughing fit. When she recovered, she gasped out, "You want to sleep with Torren for money?"

"Um, no. Well…maybe. I want him to take me out a few times first to see if this is even something I would be able to do and still live with myself."

"Are you a p-p-prostitute?" Nevada whisper screamed.

"What? No! I've never slept with anyone for money. I just dance. For people. For money." Ew, she was feeling guilty and a little judged right now. "I need the money and also…" She swallowed hard and struggled to finish her admission.

As Nevada searched her face, her eyes softened by whatever she saw there. "Also what?"

Candace's eyes burned and blurred with instant stupid tears. She shrugged. Well, what the hell? She didn't have anything to lose—that was the beauty of rock bottom. "Also, I want an adventure. I want the chance at a new friend. The chance at getting to meet someone outside of my job. Outside of my life. The chance to get out of the routine of sleep, worry over money, dance, and feel…"

"Horrible?" Nevada asked softly, brushing her fingertip over her scarred cheek.

"Yeah. Sounds silly, asking about some weird arrangement with a gorilla shifter I don't even know. But that's where I'm at."

"You want a change?"

A tear slipped to Candace's cheek, and she dashed it away quickly, gave a curt nod. "I would give anything for a change," she said thickly.

Nevada's eyes were rimmed with moisture, and her smile trembled. There was utter honesty in her voice when she murmured, "I understand." And then she scribbled an address on the back of a bookmark and slid it across the counter. "Be here at six. The boys don't like to wait on dinner. I'm sure it'll be something classy like hotdogs and beer. Dress accordingly."

Completely relieved, Candace giggled and wiped her damp cheeks again. "Sounds perfect. My shift doesn't start until nine. I'll see you in a few hours." Candace held up the bookmark and gave her one last smile. "Thanks."

Nevada's cheeks were still bright red, and she seemed to be at a loss for words as she dropped her gaze again to the stack of bookmarks. She must be very shy.

"C-C-Cinnamon?"

"Oh, my real name is Candace. Candy is what my boss used to call me. Then he changed it to Cinnamon because red hots are his favorite. Pointless story, sorry."

"C-Candace. My crew is gonna go through Hell. The boys…they're beasts. I just thought you should know before you go tonight. Are you human?"

Candace gave her a wicked smile and shook her head. "I know better than to go after a pairing with a silverback as a human. I'm a shifter, born and raised, not bitten."

"Huh," Nevada said, looking at her with slightly

narrowed eyes and her chin lifted a little higher. "Me, too."

Candace walked backward toward the door. "Oh, I've known about you Foxburgs for a long time. The boys aren't the only beasts in your crew, are they, Nevada?"

"No, they are not," the woman said just as Candace let the door swing closed behind her.

That woman might have a shyness problem, but Candace knew about foxes. Vicious little critters when given the chance. And Candace could be a vicious little critter, too.

As a rogue, she didn't usually feel safe around big, dominant shifters, but she was at a crossroads, and the silverback was more interesting than intimidating right now.

Usually everything scared her.

But right now?

Nothing did.

THREE

Nevada was acting weird.

Torren took a long drag of his beer but didn't take his eyes from the only female in the Sons of Beasts Crew. She kept looking at him, little sideways glances, and then she would look out the humongous front windows of Vyr's mansion as though waiting for something to happen.

There. She did it again. And her hands were shaking. She was never nervous around him and Vyr, so what the hell was happening to her now?

"Is there some fox war we don't know about headed our way?" he asked when she did it again.

"Fox war? Ha," she said nervously. "Vyr burned

the hair off half the den. I don't think we have to worry about them anymore. I'm gonna take the meat to the grill. Bye!" She gave him the strangest, wide-eyed look and then bustled into the kitchen.

She gathered the plate of hot dogs and burger patties out of the fridge. And now Nox was also watching her with a frown, like he smelled a rat, too. "Nevada? You okay?"

"Ha. Hahahaha. Haha. Of course, you silly gooses!"

"Geese," Vyr deadpanned from his spot in the recliner closest to the stone hearth with the blazing fire. He always took the warmest spot, the greedy dick. "The plural form would be geese. Why do you smell nervous, little vixen?"

"Me? I'm not nervous! I'm just hungry. And ready to eat. And starving."

"Is this code for you need emergency sex?" Nox asked in the most serious tone Torren had ever heard. "Because if so, we need to work on a code word or something. You're confusing me. And my dick." Nox looked at his lap and stuck out his lower lip. "My dick is confused."

"Do you ever think about the words that come from your mouth before you speak them?" Vyr asked Nox.

"No. Why would I do that?"

Nevada snorted from the kitchen, pursing her lips against a smile.

"Oh, it's funny that your mate talks before he thinks?" Vyr asked. "I'm seriously asking because I truly don't understand you two. You just…put up with him?"

"That's what the L-word is about," Nevada said. "To me, it isn't putting up with him. I get him. He makes me laugh."

"He exhausts me," Torren muttered.

"I'm going to eat seven more hamburgers than Torren tonight," Nox said, pointing the neck of his beer bottle at him. "And then you'll respect me."

"False. You'll win zero respect because I'm about to eat a dozen burgers, real-man style, and you'll be sick if you try and compete. And then Nevada won't like you anymore, and me and Vyr will be like 'finally!' and then she'll fall in *L-word* with one of us and we can kick you out of the crew. The end."

"I hate-love you," Nox growled. "And I'm gonna fight you later for saying Nevada would fall in L-word with you. She can't. You're hideous, and you're a smelly ape." Nox lifted his blond brows like he'd clearly won this round.

"Who is that?" Vyr asked, his narrowed silver eyes on the woods outside.

Torren didn't see anything yet, but he heard the rattle of a struggling engine. It was a small car with a mountain of problems under the hood if the awful screeching noises were any indication.

"It's Cinnamon!" Nox said, waving out the window at the maroon and rust-colored Volvo that struggled its way toward the circle drive. The thing coughed a cloud of black smog from the tailpipe and squeaked to a stop.

"Did you give her my address?" Vyr snarled. Whoo, the Red Dragon sounded pissed.

"No," Nox said. "I'm not trying to get eaten,

Beer."

"It's Vyr."

"Okay, Deer, and I gave Torren her cell phone number. If anyone gave her the address, it's probably him after all-night phone sex because—"

"I gave it to her," Nevada blurted out.

"What?" Vyr raged.

"I said…I…gave it to her?" Nevada's voice grew smaller with each word.

"You gave my address to a stripper? Because that's what she is, right? Cinnamon is a stripper name."

"Plus, you went to the strip club two weeks ago and saw her there," Nox said helpfully. "I followed you."

Vyr blasted a tiny fireball into the fireplace that set the logs there to blazing. "Why do you follow me everywhere?"

"Don't flatter yourself, asswipe. I follow Torren, too. And Nevada most of all. Because I'm bored! And you're my crew, and I think we're supposed to do that. Follow each other around."

"Your friendship is weird," Torren grumbled. God dangit, now he would have to talk to this girl and tell her to leave before Vyr lost his shit and Changed into the mother-freaking out-of-control Red Dragon. They were supposed to be keeping the alpha of the Sons of Beasts calm, not stressed. Nox was literally the worst man for that job.

"Vyr, you go to strip clubs?" Nevada asked.

"She's coming this way!" Nox said, jumping on the leather couch against the window and spilling his beer.

"Careful!" Vyr yelled. "And what? Are you judging me, Nevada? It's a strip club. I'm a dude."

"Did you see Cinnamon's purple, sparkly nipple tassels?" she asked without missing a beat.

Vyr clenched his fists on his thighs and emitted a low, dangerous rumble. "They were red when I went."

"With sparkles?" Nox asked from where he was still standing on the couch. "I thought she would be wearing her stripper boots but she's dressed regular."

"Yes, they had sparkles," Vyr muttered.

"What the hell?" Torren asked. "Has everyone seen this girl but me?" When he shoved Nox out of the way, his beer spilled all over the floor. Vyr yelled. Nox laughed. And Torren nearly choked on air at the hot little number sashaying her way up the stairs to the front door. Skin-tight jeans hugging her curves, a red sweater that was hiked up just enough to show a thin strip of bare skin on her hip, black snow boots to match her mittens and winter hat. She had auburn hair that she'd gathered into a messy bun just underneath her right ear, and her makeup and lipstick were dark. She had a nose piercing, just a little sparkle on her cute little nose.

"Did you say purple…tassels?" he asked dumbly, imagining her out of that little sweater. Crap, it had been too long since he'd had sex.

"I carved the hot dogs into penis shapes to make her more comfortable," Nevada announced.

Torren was getting another headache. And a boner. Which was confusing. But suddenly he understood what Nox was talking about when he said his dick was confused. Huh. Maybe he did understand his language sometimes.

He needed to get this girl out of Vyr's Mountains as soon as possible. Another rumble rattled up his throat.

Steady, HavoK.
She's not for you.
No one is.

FOUR

This was the fanciest house Candace had ever laid eyes on. Even the door knocker was a dragon head with a huge ring through its nose. Creepy and cool all at once.

Maybe she should've worn the purple sweater. That one was looser and more modest, if Torren was looking for something like that. But then he wouldn't have sent his friend to find him some steady sex if he needed a girl to bring home to Momma Kong.

The red was fine, plus it matched her lipstick. Everything was good.

To steady herself, she blew out three quick

breathes that froze in front of her face. With a
shaking hand, she knocked three times with her
mitten-clad knuckles. On the fourth, the door swung
open, and one very pissed-off red-haired giant stood
there, taking up the entire door frame.

"My house, my land, my mountains, my
territory. Fuck off."

He looked familiar. "Do…" She frowned and
angled her face to take in his features better. "Do I
know you?"

"No one does. Are you hard of hearing?"

"Enough," a deep, rumbling voice sounded from
behind the behemoth. But as the red-haired man
stepped to the side, Candace blinked hard and
arched her neck all the way back to look at the
literal giant behind the first. Oh. My. God. Torren
was the size of a redwood and was as broad as a
building. He rested both giant hands on each side of
the doorframe and resembled the sexiest letter T
she'd ever laid eyes on. His shredded arms flexed
with the motion. He wore a black T-shirt in the dead
of winter like the cold didn't bother him at all.

Right across his muscular chest was the word HavoK with a skull logo in white. Damn. He was owning the name the public gave him. Interesting. Both his arms were covered in tattoos to his knuckles. More ink showed from under the collar of his shirt and up his neck. He had a short black scruff on his chiseled jaw, and his eyes were the color of spring grass. It was such a light color, and glowing slightly. Must've been his animal color, but why was he riled up? She only got gold eyes if she was really upset, and she had good control over her animal. She could keep her human eye color if she really wanted. His hair was shaved on the sides and longer on top. It was a mess, as if he'd run his hands through it back and forth, but it was a sexy mess. It looked like he'd just rolled out of bed and didn't care about fixing it perfectly. Hotboy. Those glowing green eyes dipped down, down, down her body, pausing briefly at her little knockers and her slim hips, then with a single, slow blink, he lifted that sexy gaze back to hers. Her heart was hammering against her chest so hard he must've heard it. Bum-bum bum-bum bum-bum. Heat flooded her cheeks and her breath quickened. What was he doing to her?

When he parted those full lips, she felt like she just might pitch forward and melt against him. This man was pure seduction.

His eyes said, "Stay," but his inhuman voice said, "Fuck off."

"I…" The rest of that sentence got stuck in her throat, so Candace swallowed hard to get rid of the cotton mouth and tried again. "I was invited."

"You ain't a damn vampire. Invites don't count for as much as you think they do."

Rude man. She'd always been attracted to rude men though, so his surliness wasn't going to work like he wanted.

"Move, you beastly man," Nevada said, shoving him hard. The titan didn't move a single inch, so Nevada had to duck under his arm. "You boys are being so horrid right now!"

"I'm not!" a man called from behind the two giants blocking the door. "BJ points! We could make that a thing you know. Good behavior gets points? We could make a star chart. I'm being good so I get like four thousand BJ points."

"God dammit, Nox," Vyr said. "Shut *up*!"

"You would get negative four thousand BJ points, Beer," the man responded.

"If you call me Beer one more time—"

"Eat me!" Nox yelled.

Nevada was staring tiredly at Candace as though she disliked her life. "This. This is what I was trying to warn you about."

Candace wrapped her arms around her chest and bounced to warm herself. The breeze was making the temperature feel ten degrees colder than it really was. "Can I come in?"

"Yes," Nevada and Nox said at the exact same time Beer and Torren said, "No!"

Beer was a weird nickname, but okay.

Candace cleared her throat, exposed her neck, and avoided both dominant male's angry gazes as she stepped under Torren's massive arm. Whoo, he smelled like hotboy cologne.

"Did you just smell my armpit?" Torren asked in that deep, gravelly voice.

Chills. That's what his voice did to her. Chills rippled up her forearms. "Maybe," she muttered. "You smell good."

"I showered today."

"Congrats!" Nox said.

Candace could see him now, standing on a warn leather couch with a beer in his hand. He gave her a wicked smile and a two-fingered salute. "Good to see you again, Stripper Sally."

"Cinnamon," Torren growled from behind her.

"Actually, she goes by Candace in her real life," Nevada explained. She didn't seem shy at all anymore, and it was so strange to compare her to the girl she'd talked to in the library. They were two totally different people.

"Oh, I get it. Candy," Nox said. "Cinnamon candy. Plus forty points for the BJ jar."

"You don't get points for everything you do, you moron," Beer said.

"You just admitted we're playing, though," Nox

said, his blond brows cocked.

"No. No, no, no, I was saying if we were, there would be rules—"

"Minus fifty points for Beer being boring." Nox rolled his head back and made a snoring sound.

"I hate you," Beer muttered.

"I L-word you," Nevada told Nox.

Nox grinned. "I'm hungry for—"

"Noooo," both Torren and Beer groused.

Nox gave a Grinch smile and finished his joke with, "Nevada."

Candace giggled. She couldn't help it. These boys were a mess, but they were interesting and kind of funny. When she looked up at Torren, he was watching her lips.

"Nice laugh," he said, "for a stripper."

"Whatever that means," Candace popped off. "Rude."

Torren frowned, his dark eyebrows drawing down deeply, like she'd confused him. Perhaps he wasn't used to someone calling him out on his bad manners.

"You don't smell that sad," he said, crossing his arms over his massive chest.

"Because I'm not."

"I thought you would be all sickly and pathetic."

"Again. Rude. I dance at night. I do what I have to do to make money. You're hiring a girl to have sex with you, so you can't judge. You aren't a saint either, Torren."

When she said his name, he flinched as though he'd been slapped, and his eyes went round.

"Buuuuuurn," Nox murmured. "Called out by some five-foot-two wildcat, meow." He clawed up his fingers and hissed, and in the kitchen, Nevada laughed.

Torren jammed a meaty middle finger at Nox, his eyes never leaving Candace. "I didn't hire you, nor am I interested."

"Lie," Nox said, jumping in the air and landing on his butt on the couch cushion.

Torren huffed an animalistic breath and glanced at Nox with the meanest frown before he gave his attention to Candace again. "I wouldn't hire you for sex if you were the last—"

"Also lie," Nox said. "You're lying right now. I can hear it."

"And furthermore, you couldn't handle a man like me in the bedroom—"

"Also probably a lie because she's a stripper."

"Shut up, Nox!" Torren bellowed. In a flurry of blurred movement, Torren made it all the way across the room and blasted Nox in the jaw. The speed and accuracy and power behind that hit made Candace jump. Nox wasn't defenseless, though. It was as if the grizzly shifter had been ready, because he was already up, blasting Torren in the face right back. There was a crack of a broken nose and then both monster men went to the floor, all locked up.

"Shouldn't we stop them?" Candace yelled at Beer, who stood by the fireplace with his hands on his hips, looking at them in disgust.

"They do this all the time," Nevada explained, ignoring the fight as she chopped up a tomato. "We're having hamburgers and hotdogs today," she said, lifting her voice over the splintering sound of the end table they'd just smashed through. "That probably sounds weird because it's cold and snowy outside and not hamburger weather, but the boys are really good at grilling, and we don't have a lot of money between us."

Torren took a hit to the ribs and grunted in pain. And then something horrifying happened. The red-haired man inhaled and parted his lips, then blew a tiny sphere of fire, no bigger than a golf ball, at Torren, who was going to town on Nox's face. When it hit him in the back of the neck, the man yelled in pain and pulled off Nox, his hand gripping the burn like that would make it better.

And it hit her.

Beer.

Vyr.

This was the Red Dragon.

Holy. Shit.

Candace backed slowly to the door. She was in the lair of the mother-freaking out-of-control dragon shifter who was wanted for shifter prison. Who had burned all of Covington just six months ago. Who had burned half the damn fox den here. How had she been so dumb? Of course, this was Vyr. She'd been so focused and nervous about Torren, she hadn't paid enough attention to the real danger.

"Where are you going?" Nox asked, blood streaming from his nose.

"Uh, I just remembered I already have dinner plans."

Vyr narrowed his eyes, but now they were terrifying. They were churning silver with elongated pupils. Dragon, dragon, dragon, shit, shit, shit.

Pain behind her eyes nearly blinded her, and she doubled over.

"Whoa," Vyr said. "What do we have here? Wildcat, indeed. Pretty kitty. Bad kitty. What got you into stripping?" He was approaching slowly, hunting her, stalking her. Candace's back hit the door. She'd convinced herself over the last few days that she wasn't scared of anything, but in this moment, she knew she'd been wrong to be so careless. To think she was safe from anything.

"Stop," she pleaded.

"You haven't done this long. Not long enough to smell sad yet, huh, pretty kitty? Two years." Vyr angled his head from side to side, keeping her trapped in his gaze. The pain was so bad in her head she went to her knees.

"Stop," Torren rumbled.

"Dead."

"Please stop," she begged, her eyes burning with tears.

"Your dad."

A sob wrenched from her. *Dad. Dad, Dad, Dad, I miss you, Dad.*

Torren blasted Vyr across the face with a closed fist, and the pain faded instantly as the gorilla shifter picked him up by the shirt and ran him into the wall. He slammed the dragon shifter against it so hard the wood splintered around his body.

"You want to die?" Vyr yelled.

"Do you? You're being a dick. She's crying, man. Save your evil bullshit for someone who deserves it. Stay out of her fuckin' head!"

Tears streaming down her face, Candace

stumbled upward and yanked open the door. She fled down the stairs and to her car as fast as she could. Vyr was a monster. The Red Dragon could read minds. He could pull her memories right from her. And without her consent.

She slipped on the way to her car, almost fell, but righted herself and pulled open the door. Crying so hard, she jammed her key into the ignition with shaking hands and turned it over. Nothing. Shit! She tried again and again and again. Of course, her car would break down now when she needed a quick getaway.

Of course!

This was so perfect. The perfect comment on her life. Anytime she needed anything, actually *needed* something, everything fell apart even worse.

She rested her forehead against the steering wheel and wrapped her arms around her stomach. And then she just…broke down.

The door opened, and the car rocked with a great weight as someone sat in the passenger's seat. She didn't even care if Vyr was here to finish her off. "If you're going to eat me, make it fast," she said with a pathetic sniffle.

"Eating out girls isn't as fun when they're crying. Or so I assume," Torren said.

Relief flooded her body, and she sagged against the wheel. Rolling her head, she angled her face to him.

"Your make-up is shot, woman. You look like a raccoon." Torren was squished into the passenger's seat of her tiny Volvo, and his knees were nearly up to his chest.

"Well, you look like you're in a clown car."

He stared at her blankly for a three-count, but then his lips curved up into a smile. He chuckled.

Which made her giggle.

His chuckle got a little louder.

And she laughed.

"God," he muttered, running his hand through his dark hair and shaking his head at whatever he was staring at out the window.

When she followed his gaze, Nox was pelvic thrusting against the big picture window of the mansion.

Torren sighed. "Are you okay?"

"No. My life is circling the toilet, and I came to see about having sex with a man for money. And then I met the Red Dragon and he took memories from me. I feel violated."

"Yeah, he shouldn't have done that. He forgets sometimes."

"Forgets what?"

Torren arched his blazing bright green gaze to hers. "He forgets to feel. He's cold. It wasn't always like that, but he's complicated."

"Um…thank you."

"For what?"

"For making him stop. That was a huge risk you took." She gripped the wheel and stared out at the snowflakes that had slowly started falling. The idea of how powerful all three men were was intimidating. "Because he blew a fireball. In his human form. That's fucked up."

"You have a filthy mouth."

"It's not going to change with you

complaining."

"Didn't say I was complaining. Were you really going to sleep with me for money?"

"Maybe. I don't know. I had a plan."

"Tell me the plan."

She frowned at the sexy stranger beside her. "Okay. I wasn't just going to jump into bed with you. I was going to negotiate. I was going to make you take me out on dates. At least three so we could see if we could be friends with…you know."

"Benefits?"

"Yeah. Um…I'm a tiger."

"In the sack?" he asked with a hopeful tone to his voice.

"No," she said with a giggle. "I mean I'm a tiger shifter. Not a pretty white one, though. I'm an orange one. My stripes are thin so I look solid orange from a distance other than my white points. I look like my dad. He was mostly orange, too. My mom was a white tiger, but I don't remember her much. She left when I was three, so it was just me and my dad. I always liked looking like him and not her." She shook her head and laughed nervously. "I don't know why I just told you that."

"He died?"

She bit her bottom lip and nodded. "Last year. Still feels new sometimes, though."

"Pretty kitty. Broken kitty."

"Not broken. You just met me during a hard chapter of my story."

Torren smiled sadly. "Same."

"At least you have a crew," she said, because positivity had always been her thing. Look for the bright sides. There was always at least one.

"You're alone?"

She nodded. "It was part of the appeal of trying to be your friend."

"With benefits."

"Yeah. That was just a bonus. You're kind of hot."

Torren looked surprised and then belted out a single laugh. Was he blushing now? She definitely was.

"I got a problem with my animal, but sex won't

fix me. Nox shouldn't have asked you. Nothing is gonna fix me."

"Because you're HavoK?"

He jerked his gaze to hers. "You researched me?"

"Hell, yeah. I want to know the type of man I'm prostituting myself for." She cracked a smile so he would know she was joking, but he only frowned deeper.

"You would hate being friends with me, and I would terrorize you in the bedroom. I'm not a man you want to make a deal with. But your car probably has a dozen things that need to be worked on, it's cold, and Vyr has the burgers on the grill by now. This ain't a date because, trust me when I say, you don't want that with me. But how about you spend the evening with a few fuck-ups and the Red Dragon?"

"Will Vyr hurt me?"

Torren shook his head somberly. "I won't let him." Torren shoved open his door with a *creeeaaak* and got out. Then he strode around the front of her car, pulled open her door, and offered his hand. "I promise you, Wildcat. You're safe."

You're safe. That was the best combination of words in the whole wide world. And she'd listened to his voice when he uttered them. He'd been telling the truth. She was safe with him. He was a beast and could be swift with violence as she'd seen when he'd fought Nox and Vyr. But with her? He was being careful. He was being gentle. He would make sure she survived the night.

And she trusted him—this stranger. He'd gone after the Red Dragon to keep him out of her head. He'd earned that trust in just seconds.

"What do you say? You want to have a non-date with me? You want to pretend to be friends without benefits just for the night?"

She slid her hand against Torren's palm and allowed him to help her out of her car. "Yeah. That sounds like just the kind of adventure I was looking for."

FIVE

"Your swan looks cold," Candace pointed out.

"Not my swan," Torren said, leading the way around the half-frozen pond toward a glass-encased patio off the back of the mansion.

"Nox's?"

"Nox is going to eat it at some point. Nevada and I have bets going on how long Mr. Diddles will last."

Candace giggled. "You named him Mr. Diddles?"

"His name was supposed to be Fergus or some fancy-schmancy name like that, but Nox saw him humping that duck statue over there on the edge of the pond and re-named him. That idiot came in and ruined everything. Vyr is going to burn him at some point. Nevada and I have bets on that, too."

Candace gulped and jogged to catch up with Torren's long strides, her boots crunching in the snow. "Does Vyr eat a lot of people?"

"Yep. And don't worry about the swan. I rigged him up a house with a heater." Torren pointed to a tiny replica of the mansion with an opening and an orange glowing light emanating from within. "The fucker is just too dumb to stay in it for more than thirty minutes at a time. I think it likes the cold.

Mr. Diddles was watching them ghost the edge of his pond with one suspicious, beady eye. Candace didn't like birds that much, but maybe it was the tiger in her. "You built that swan house?"

"Mmm hmm."

"Okay, that's extra sexy-points because a handyman is a sexy man."

Torren came to an abrupt stop and turned to her, his head cocked. "Really?"

"Umm, yes. I can barely put together a

bookshelf that is mostly assembled and includes directions. I'm not mechanically minded at all." She came to a stop beside him and looked up. "Where did you learn how to build something like that? It's beautiful. And thoughtful."

"Not thoughtful. Vyr loves that stupid oversized goose, and if he dies, Vyr will Change and burn everything to the ground and get us all arrested and probably eat like…half the town. I probably should've said that last part first because it's the most important part, but…you know…I don't want to go to shifter prison if I can avoid it." He cracked a stunning smile. "I hear the food there sucks."

"No bananas?" she teased.

"Oh, she's got monkey jokes."

After Candace curtsied magnanimously, Torren did something that shocked her. He ruffled her hair and shoved her gently. "You're gonna be annoying. I can already tell." He sauntered away, but the way he'd said it made her smile. There was affection in his voice. Or amusement perhaps. And when he turned and flashed her a smile over his shoulder, something electric snapped inside of her and made her gasp.

Torren walked backward and dragged his flirty gaze down and then up her body again. "You coming?"

"Only if you make me."

"Make you come?" he asked, his smile growing brighter and eyes churning with naughtiness. "I'd wreck you for everyone else. You don't want that, Wildcat. You want to be able to settle with mediocre sex someday."

"Cocky," she accused, following him step-for-step.

Torren glanced down at his crotch and gave a nod. "Yep. Big cocky."

"You're gonna be really annoying," she said, stealing his words. "I can already tell." Candace bent down and scooped up a handful of snow, shaped it into a ball, and chucked it at him.

Torren ducked it easily. "You throw like a stripper."

"Oh, my gosh, how many times are you going to

bring that up?"

Torren bent easily and scooped snow in his giant hand, then packed a giant snowball. "At least a dozen times a day. That's how I plan to chase you off, don't you know? Shame you for your shameful profession."

"You're being mean," she said, jumping out of the way of his snowball.

"Haven't you heard about silverbacks? We're the worst."

"All of you are assholes?"

"Every last one."

"Even Kong?"

Torren stopped walking backward and frowned. "My dad's the only good silverback."

Candace smiled sadly and admitted, "Sometimes I think my dad was the only good tiger."

They stood there looking at each other, neither one saying what they'd just admitted. Each had told the other they weren't good. That the good in their family had stopped with their fathers.

Torren straightened his spine and inhaled deeply. "Smells like dinner is on. What do you drink? We have cheap beer or tap water."

"No fancy wine in the mansion?" she asked.

Torren's lip twitched, but not in amusement. It wasn't a smile. "Look around the house when you go inside. Really look. We aren't living fancy here, Wildcat." Torren dropped his gaze to the snow, then back to her for just a moment before he spun and strode toward the enclosed back porch.

Huh. Candace followed and opened the door that had banged closed behind him. And then she did as he asked. She really looked around. The porch was much warmer, protected from the breeze by windowed walls, but the table was nothing more than a cheap, fold-out card table that sat six. The chairs were mismatched plastic ones and two had duct tape on the legs. A blue cooler that was old and scratched sat by a charcoal grill that probably cost thirty bucks at the general store. Vyr and Nox were pulling burgers off and Nevada was setting out a tray of tomatoes, pickles, and lettuce. There were heaters above attached at each corner, but none were turned on and everyone was wearing their jackets.

"Can I help?" she asked Nevada.

"Yeah, you wanna grab napkins and a knife for the mustard?" she muttered as she began opening the condiments on the table. "Oh! And grab the strawberries?"

"Sure," Candace murmured, making her way inside. She could see the great room from here and really took it in. The couch and loveseat were red and brown and didn't match. They were made of tattered, old leather with rips on some of the seats. The end tables looked like they came from thrift stores, and there was nothing decorating the walls or the mantle over the stone hearth. The kitchen was beautiful with polished granite countertops and hand-scraped wooden cabinets. But when she opened the cupboard near the fridge, it had plastic cups from barbecue restaurants and paper plates.

"See?" Torren asked from right behind her.

It should've startled her, how quiet he could

sneak up on her, but for some reason she didn't even jump. Her body reacted differently to the sound of his deep, snarly voice. It sent a hard shiver up her spine, and she didn't turn around.

"I like that reaction. I like that I can make you tremble," he said, even closer to her.

His warmth radiated onto her back, and when he brushed her arm with the tips of his fingers, she automatically exhaled and melted backward against his solid stone chest. It was like resting against a wall, but one that made her feel safe somehow.

A deep, satisfied rumble rattled from his chest against her shoulder blades.

"You said you would ruin me for other men," she whispered, her eyes closed so she could feel his fingertips running through her hair. "What if I'm already ruined?"

"What are you doing?" he asked, his voice nearly inhuman. "You're calling the animal. It's a dangerous game you're playing."

She responded with a purr and arched her back, pressing her backside against his erection. Big boy.

His hand gripped her hip to keep her in place, and his other hand tightened in her hair and pulled her head back, exposing her neck.

"You would be so easy to hurt," he whispered.

When Torren sucked hard on her neck, Candace moaned, completely lost in the moment. She reached behind her and gripped the leg of his jeans, begging him to come closer. And he did. He shoved her against the counter and ground his erection against her ass so hard, she thirsted for him. Rough silverback, he would make her feel good and forget about the bad parts of her life for a little while. He could offer her a beautiful escape.

He moved faster, grinding on her through their clothes, and when he slid his fingers through hers and pinned her hand onto the counter, she wanted to beg him to take her somewhere private so he could finish them both.

But he backed off of her so fast, she startled. One second he was there with her, connecting, touching her, warming her, and the next…he was across the kitchen, grabbing two glasses of water off the counter. Without a single look back at her, he disappeared down the short hallway to the back porch. The door slammed so hard she jumped.

What the ever-lovin' hell just happened?

Her body was still on fire from his touch and, dumbly, she tried to recall what Nevada had asked her to get. Plates? Okay. Mayo? Yes. Good, she wasn't completely useless right now.

But when she stumbled out onto the porch, Nevada frowned at the plates and murmured, "Strawberries, napkins, and a knife. That's not even close." And then she arched her gaze over to Torren, who was shoving himself into the small space between Vyr and Nox.

"Sorry," Candace murmured. She spun around and made her way back into the kitchen, gathered the stuff she was supposed to bring, and hurried back outside.

The others were already seated, and the only empty chair was one next to Nevada with silver duct tape on the leg. Torren was squished between Nox and Vyr, and both of them were giving him matching what-the-fuck looks.

Dumb boy. He was making Candace feel like she had cooties. It's not like she needed to sit by him anyway, especially if he was going to act weird.

She sat down beside Nevada and scooped strawberries onto her plate and then onto the fox shifter's plate. She shoved the bowl over to the boys' side without making eye contact with Torren. Her cheeks were on fire. It wasn't her way to be embarrassed, but he'd bolted so fast it had to be her…right? But it was good they hadn't taken the little romp in the kitchen any further because they were supposed to have three dates before she made a decision on the benefits part of this friendship. She couldn't afford to just jump into a bad decision with a man. She wanted to get to know him a little first, figure out if he was a D-bag and would bail.

They ate in silence for a few minutes before Candace reached for a conversation starter. "Why have a mansion with old couches and paper plates?"

Vyr and Torren ignored her, but Nox pulled out

a little book from his back pocket with bent, worn pages and a title on the front cover that read *Manners & Shit*.

He flipped through a few pages, popped a strawberry into his maw, and read aloud. "When you have a dinner guest, you should answer their questions with politeness and honesty. Huh." He scooted his chair back loudly and stood, clinking a plastic knife against his beer bottle. *Clunk, clunk, clunk.* "Okay, I'll go. Vyr was rich, but the government froze his accounts when he burned Covington and ate like a dozen gorillas and lions. Torren is greedy with his money, I'm between bounty hunting jobs, and Nevada hasn't been paid but once by her library job, so…paper plates. And no heat. And we all pitch in to keep the lights on and keep this fine cuisine on the table."

Vyr and Torren were chewing their burgers and glaring at Nox.

"What?" Nox asked, sitting back down.

"Why do you have a book on manners?" Vyr asked around a bite of food.

"I don't know this shit, and I'm trying to be a good crew member because Nevada gets horny when I'm polite." Nox kicked Torren under the table.

Torren yelped a curse, then shoved Nox so hard the plastic leg of his chair broke and he went down hard.

"Idiots," Vyr muttered. "We're out of duct tape. Now you get to stand."

"I hate you," Nox whispered.

"I hate you more," Torren whispered back.

They glared at each other another few seconds before Nox whispered, "You're my best friend."

"Stop." Torren shook his head and rolled his eyes and looked so mad that Candace had to purse her lips against a smile.

"It's not funny," Torren said, glaring at her.

"I know. I'm not laughing."

"Well," Torren growled, "you look like you're laughing."

"You two have a very cute bromance."

"See?" Nox crowed from where he was eating

his burger on the ground now. "Even she sees our chemistry."

"Well, she's a stripper, so—"

Splat.

Candace gasped and clapped her hand over her mouth. She couldn't believe she'd just thrown a mayo-covered tomato slice at him. It was sliding slowly down his cheek, and when he turned a wild, green-eyed gaze on her, he looked enraged.

Beside her, Nevada was giggling as quietly as she could, which was making Candace have the giggles, too.

"Stop bringing up that I'm a stripper. If you have to call me something, call me a dancer."

"Well, you dance for money, soooo…"

"Whoa, judgey judgerton," Nox said from somewhere on the other side of the table. "Manners and Shit, page fourteen. 'Try to be open minded with dinner guests to make them feel more comfortable in your space.' And besides, you can't say anything. So she dances for money? You fight— Oooow!" Nox howled when Torren kicked at him.

Vyr sat up straighter and stopped chewing. "What were you about to say?"

"Nothing," Nox ground out.

"No, you said something about fighting. T, are you fighting?"

"Manners and Shit, page fifteen," Torren rumbled. "'Give the guest a tour of the house.'"

"I don't see that on page fifteen," Nox said over the sound of rustling pages.

Torren was already carrying his empty paper plate inside, though.

"Am I supposed to follow him?" Candace asked, confused.

"Uh, I think so," Nevada answered.

Vyr was glaring at the ground where Nox was eating his dinner.

"What?" Nox asked around a full mouth.

"I hate this crew," Vyr muttered.

"You lied!" Nevada sounded so happy right now.

Everything was confusing. Candace grabbed her

empty plate and followed Torren inside for some mansion tour she was pretty sure he used as an excuse to escape Vyr's questions.

Letting him off the hook, she said, "You don't have to give me the tour. I have to go to work soon, anyway." Candace pulled the sleeves of her sweater down over her hands and forced a smile as he turned toward her in the kitchen. "It was really weird eating with you and your crew. But…it was a good weird. You have something special here, Torren. Protect it." She gave him a little wave, and turned for the door.

"Wait." Torren scrubbed his hand down his short, dark beard. "My sister. She's why I don't share my money. Or much of it anyway. She's the reason I'm not bankrolling us here."

Candace fidgeted with a loose thread on her sweater. "What do you mean?"

He twitched his head to the side. "I'll show you." Turning, he led her down a hallway to the last door on the left. Torren pushed open the door and watched her face—for what, she didn't know.

The bedroom was done in dark colors. Dark brown walls and a navy-blue comforter on a queen-sized mattress on the ground. There was no end table or even a bed frame. There was no dresser, only four piles of clothes stacked neatly against the wall. On the wall hung a single picture. It was a black and white of four people. Torren was younger in it, twenty perhaps and lankier than he was now. He had his arm slung around a dark-haired girl with a pixie cut. She had the biggest grin on her face as she looked right at the camera. Torren was smiling down at her, and beside them, a giant, short-haired man stood behind a petite blond woman with his arms around her shoulders. They were both looking at Torren and the girl.

"Your sister?" Candace guessed.

Torren lifted his hands and began to sign something, shocking her that he knew American Sign Language. She couldn't do more than sign the simple alphabet, but he was speaking without words, and his hands were poetry.

When he was finished, she asked, "What did

you say?"

"I said this is my sister, Genevieve, and she was born deaf. She's smart, brave, and loyal, and she's my favorite person. And when she got old enough, she wanted to be a part of a family group. Her gorilla wanted the big family. But her silverback alpha was awful and so were the females. They took her life savings away from her. She was supposed to get cochlear implants. They have a good chance of working for her, making it so she can hear. Not like you and me, but it would still be something very important to her. She would be able to hear her mate tell her 'I love you.' She wants to hear his voice so badly. So, a lot of Damon's Mountains and her Red Havoc Crew have been working to save money for her, but it's really expensive."

"How expensive?"

"Shifters don't get insurance because we aren't supposed to get sick. She has to pay forty thousand dollars out of pocket."

"Oh my gosh," Candace murmured, dropping down to sit on the edge of Torren's mattress.

Torren joined her and pulled out a metal ammo box from beside his bed. He glanced at her once, his eyes churning that bright inhuman green, before he opened it and showed her what was inside. There were neat stacks of money, mostly fives and tens.

"You're a stripper. You can't judge. You have issues just like me so we're safe."

Candace nodded. Safe. That felt right.

"I have to fight. The gorilla is fucked up. Nox and Vyr think it's because I don't have a family group under me, but that's not it. I was always fucked up, even when I was a kid. I can't control the Changes. I'm getting worse. The only thing that steadies me is fighting. I have to fight all the time. I hide it from Vyr because we're supposed to be perfectly behaved right now. We can't draw any attention. But I can't be perfect because I never was. I can't even pretend. I'm a monster."

"You're not," Candace said, shaking her head.

"I am. Best you understand that right away if you want to be friends. You dance for money. I fight. I don't judge you. I like to give you shit because you have funny reactions, but who am I to say you live your life wrong? Mine is a disaster."

"You have more going for you than you realize, HavoK."

"Everything I tell you stays in here. Swear it."

"I swear. I'm good at keeping secrets."

Torren drew his knees up to his chest and rested his arms on them. He searched her eyes before he said low, "I'm trying to stay sane long enough to help my sister get those cochlear implants. I want her to hear my voice before Vyr has to put me down. She's what keeps me going."

Ooooh, so Torren was much deeper than she thought at first glance. He wasn't just being silly with Nox with his fighting and jokes. He wasn't just this big, tattooed gym rat. He had layers, and the ones he'd just exposed were kind of beautiful. Still, he believed he would be put down. Only shifters who were really bad off were put down by their alphas, but Torren seemed strong, steady, and capable. "But you seem fine."

"I've Changed six times today."

"Oh my goodness," she murmured, feeling sick to her stomach. Changes hurt. They hurt badly. Torren seemed in control now, but clearly, he wasn't. His gorilla forced a Change that often? She couldn't even imagine her tiger betraying her like that. She Changed once a week, and it was on her terms, when she wanted to. "How can I help?"

"You can't. No one can." Suddenly, Torren yanked his shirt over his head and bunched it tightly in his hands. He swallowed hard and turned so she could see his back. The top of his shoulders and the back of his neck were tattooed, but the rest of his back was free of ink. There was a massive birthmark that stretched like the milky way from his left hip up his back to the edge of his tattoos. "I'm marked, like my father was. It's called the Mark of the Kong. I'm supposed to be the silverback leading the biggest family group with the best genetics. I'm supposed to be Kong now, but my dad gave me the choice. I could take my place with my people and rule them, or I could be like him. I could buck tradition and live the life I chose."

"What would you have to do as Kong?"

Torren squeezed the shirt until his knuckles turned white. "Breed a bunch of females. My dad was supposed to sire this generation of monsters like me. But he chose my mom, and they only had me and my sister. As soon as the gorillas figured out I was marked, the pressure was on. I'm supposed to make the monster gorillas for the next generation. An army. That's how they work. Family groups aren't these big loving crews. They have their intentions on child rearing for the sake of numbers. I always wanted a baby… Fuck. Let's go. I don't want to talk anymore." Torren stood suddenly and walked to the door where he turned. "It's just I wanted what my dad found, and I chose wrong. I went all in, thinking I would find a single mate like my parents, but it never happened and now I'm messed up." He held her for a few more seconds with eyes that had muddied to a forest green and were begging her understanding. "I'm going crazy, and I chose wrong. I can't be your friend. Relationships make me unstable, and I have to make it to my sister's surgery. You understand? I have to keep steady enough until then. I can't do this. I'm sorry."

Candace's heart physically hurt for him. He was carrying more burden than any man she'd ever met. And she had the bone-deep feeling not even his crew knew how much weight he was shouldering.

I'm sorry. He'd apologized for not being able to give her friendship. He was admitting he was stretched too thin. Torren didn't realize it, but that was a mark of a good man. He wasn't one to build up peoples' hopes, or lead anyone on. He knew what he was capable of, and though he'd looked gutted to admit it, he'd told her upfront he couldn't be fixed.

And now she would go back to being alone, and he would go back to being in a crew, but still alone with the burden of a too-short life.

"I'm sorry, too," she murmured.

SIX

"Well, that sucked," Carl complained as he threw the curtain back on the dressing room. "You were like a landed fish flopping around out there! How is anyone supposed to get turned on by that? Your eyes were completely dead. Are you high?"

"What? No! I'm just having an off night." Candace slathered on another layer of glitter blush to her cheeks and plumped her lips with fire-engine red lipstick. She hated the way she looked all done up for work. She was like this doll someone had given a little girl who wanted to try make-up, and the little girl had made a rainbow mess all over her face. It was part of the job though—a part that was necessary for her. If she looked into the mirror and saw her real face here, she wouldn't be able to go back out there and do what she needed to do.

A hundred and fifty dollars is what she needed to make, but Torren's story about his sister had been swirling around in her head all night. She wished she was rich and could help. She wished she could do something. She desperately wanted him to live long enough to tell his sister he loved her. Anything less would be too tragic to bear.

Why did she care so deeply already? Candace put another layer of eyeliner on in the mirror. It was one of those old-fashioned ones with the lightbulbs around the edge. Carl had tried to make the dressing room glamorous, but mostly it looked cheap and smelled of sadness. Oh, she'd known exactly what Torren had been talking about with that. Doris had been working here damn near ten years, and her eyes were dead every night. She went through the motions like a trained corpse. Currently, she was sitting in the last chair, staring at herself in the mirror, not moving. She was up next, but she'd looked close to tears all night.

"I can't," she whispered.

"What did you say?" Carl asked.

Doris arched an empty gaze to Carl. There was a rim of tears in her eyes. "I said I—"

"She wants me to do her number," Candace cut in. "We've been working on it. Doris had a bad day, and she wants a little break. It's okay. I've got this."

Carl narrowed his eyes. "Fine. Doris, you can take the rest of the night off. That was your last dance. Cinnamon, don't fuck this up. At least look alive out there." He hustled out of the room, and the curtain swished closed behind him.

"You didn't have to do that," Doris murmured.

"They gotta job opening at Essie's Pantry," Candace said fast before the other two girls got back from their dance. The music was blaring, and she had to repeat it for Doris to hear. "I've been looking at switching things up. I won't go after that job if you want it."

"But then *you* won't get out of here," Doris said in a vacant voice. "You'll end up just like me."

"I'll find another way."

Doris huffed a laugh and shook her head, returned her attention to her reflection. "You and I both know that grocery store salary won't touch the instant cash we could make here."

"But is the cash worth the cost?" Candace asked.

Doris didn't answer. Instead she pulled her fake eyelashes off and tossed them into the wastebasket beside her, then pulled her duffle bag over her shoulder and strode for the door.

"Aren't you going to change? It's early enough to grab dinner somewhere?"

"No, honey. I'm going home. I have a microwave dinner with my name on it, and it don't care that I'm dressed in hoochie clothes." She gave a little half-assed smile and left the way Carl did.

Tonight sucked. Candace had been struggling with this job for a while, but seeing Doris so sad made her afraid that if she didn't change her stars, she really would end up like her. Ten years in, and she'd be completely jaded by men and the way they looked at girls like her and Doris. The way they treated them. Oh, some were nice enough, but Candace didn't do lap dances, and sometimes men got angry when they drank at the bar here. Sometimes they got rough or said cruel things to try to shame her into dancing just for them.

What was she doing here? Dad would've rolled over in his grave if he knew she was paying his medical bills like this. She was so far from the girl her dad has raised, and the shame she tried so hard to keep at bay reared its ugly head. Heat crept up her neck and made a pit stop in her cheeks, and carefully, she turned her face away from the mirror.

"You're up," Carl yelled through the curtain over the cheering from the main room.

A hundred and fifty dollars to dance half naked, and for some reason she'd felt less cheap when she'd considered sleeping with Torren for money. Why? She'd never been tempted to sleep with a boy who wasn't serious about her. Why now? Was it desperation for money? For a friend? For a change? For him?

"Cinnamon!" Carl yelled.

She dashed a knuckle under her eyes just in case a tear had escaped, then stood and inhaled deeply, steeling herself to put on the show so she could pay her electric bill. She could do this, same as every other night.

"Coming," she murmured.

SEVEN

Torren was at the bar getting Vyr a beer—ha, Vyr a beer, a poet as fuck—when he heard a man call for Cinnamon. God, he hated that name. Candace was much prettier and suited her better. Her real name. Real suited real, and there was something about that woman that had drawn up into fine focus when they'd been talking in his room.

Vyr was a douche for ordering him to come here.

"You don't do the alpha shit right," he mumbled as he handed Vyr his drink and sat down beside him, close enough to the stage to touch it. "You're only supposed to make orders for the good of the crew."

"Yeah, I don't care. I never wanted to be alpha, so if you and Nox and Nevada are going to make me do this, I'm going to run it how I want. Now shhh. It's starting, and I don't want you to miss the best part. Oh." Vyr slid a silver-eyed glare at Torren. "And I order you not to Change."

There was steel in the Red Dragon's voice, and inside of Torren, something awful happened. The gorilla roared as he shrank into a ball, bringing an instant wave of pain to Torren's body. The silverback side of him didn't like to be controlled. He fought everything.

Doubled over, Torren gritted his teeth as the music started. But the second he saw her—Candace—the pain went away.

She looked so different from the girl he'd met earlier. And it wasn't just the purple, sparkly eyeshadow or the shining glitter that adorned her body. It wasn't her dark hair in cascading waves down the middle of her back or the heavy eyeliner. It wasn't the black, lacy bra or matching panties or the red satin high heels with a trail of cheap rhinestones winding around the sharp heel. It was her eyes that looked different. She'd flipped a switch.

Torren would recognize that look anywhere. He saw it often enough when he looked at his reflection in the mirror after a fight. Face all bloodied, he would stare at himself and wait for the vacant look to go away.

He could tell right now that Candace didn't see anything as she made her way to the stage, shoulders back like she had all the pride and confidence in the world.

There were wolf-whistles and cheers around them, but Torren ignored the animals in the smoky bar. His focus was on her. Because he didn't give a single shit that she was a dancer. He really didn't. If this profession made her happy, or even if she was good with it and secure in her place in the world, he would be fine with it, too. He was open-minded. She hadn't smelled sad earlier, so he'd expected to come in here and see her smiling and working the crowd. What he hadn't expected was the grim set to her mouth, like she was clenching her teeth, or the ghosts in her eyes as she leapt up onto the pole and spun around it like a goddamn acrobat. Her eyes focused on nothing, as if she'd checked out and was going through the motions.

Torren angled his face and narrowed his eyes, studying her. She looked confident enough in her movements, completely owned the stage, so why had she gone empty on the inside?

He looked around at the men, bobbing their heads to the pounding bass beat. Tongues slid across teeth, and buddies leaned over to each other and said vulgar things. A dozen or so men crowded the edge of the stage. And he got it. Candace was the prettiest girl in here by far. Hell, she was the prettiest girl he'd ever seen, dressed like this or dressed in her skinny jeans and red sweater and snow boots.

The men were reaching for her, and she played the crowd, danced for them, but avoided their hands when they wanted to put money in her panties.

Good girl. If they touched her, Torren was going to rip their fucking heads off, one by one.

He tossed back his beer and downed it.

"Don't Change," Vyr rumbled in that dragon voice that terrified normies, but not Torren. Vyr was his best friend. He wouldn't hurt him. Even out of control, the Red Dragon had always saved him from his burning fire.

When Torren clenched his empty beer bottle, it broke in his hand. It stung, but he ignored it. Warmth trickled down his fingers, but still he ignored it. He couldn't take his eyes off Candace. God, she was so fucking beautiful. So sexy. She was a really good dancer, better than this place deserved. Whoever had choreographed this had real talent. She was flexible and naturally graceful. She wasn't just throwing her hips around either. She was on the pole with skill, then back down to the floor, doing moves that should've only made sense in some fancy-ass ballet, but it worked with this hard-hitting rock song somehow.

"She's beautiful, ain't she?" the guy a couple

seats down asked. When Torren didn't answer, he tried again, louder. "She's a beauty, ain't she?"

"Yeah," Torren growled out.

"Total prude though, so if you have plans on getting a private dance from that one, she won't do it. She never gives lap dances, much less goes back to that private room. No one's allowed to touch her either. I think it's part of her show. She gets everyone addicted, thinking they can be the one to entice her to be bad. She only ever gets the money the boys leave on the stage. Shame. She's the star here. She could make four times what she does, easy. Fuck, I would pay her four times if she would give in just once." The man had long greasy hair and yellow teeth, and though his words were friendly enough, there was a predator in his smile.

Torren scanned the rest of the guys in the room, and they all wore matching expressions as they watched Candace dance.

"Don't. Change." Vyr was getting on his damn nerves with the orders.

By the time the song ended, his body was

humming with the power of the subdued silverback inside of him. He wanted to go King Kong and let the monster have him, rip this place apart brick-by-brick. He wanted to bury these guys for even looking at Candace like they owned her. Fuckers didn't understand. This kitty was wild, and men couldn't *own* wild things.

She was a prude? Nah, she was just smart to keep their paws off her. She was giving up an income she was clearly desperate for so she could keep herself intact. So she could keep the good things about herself. So she could survive this. He imagined some people didn't. Not really. They kept breathing, sure, but a profession like this would make them numb inside. They would flip that switch a thousand too many times and one day not remember how to turn it back on. They would stay numb. Candace was trying to be okay. These assholes didn't care about that, though. To them, these girls were playthings. They were only here on this earth to be stared at, whistled at, grabbed at.

Fucking humans. If they even knew what

resided inside of Candace, they wouldn't be staring at her like they had the upper hand. Her tiger could end any of their lives with zero effort. And look at her…eyes still soft. They hadn't changed color at all. She smelled like fur and perfume like she was trying to cover her animal scent, but Torren could smell a big cat shifter from anywhere.

She was in such tight control. Sexy Wildcat. They were opposite. He couldn't manage his animal at all, and this woman had learned to tame the damn beast inside of her. And she wasn't submissive either. That tiger wasn't hiding. She was like a trained animal in the circus, and Candace was the best ringmaster he'd ever seen.

And suddenly, he had a moment where he wished she could save him. Where he wished she could train his silverback like she'd trained her tiger. Ring master, ring master, he wished to God she could be his ring master.

"Hey," the guy next to him called to Candace as she bent to pick up the money that was scattered around the edge of the stage.

She'd used those same hands to scoop snow to throw at him earlier. She'd used those same hands to play. He'd pinned that hand to the counter as he'd pressed his dick into her back and nearly came just from touching her. And now she was picking up money from these assholes. How had she gotten here?

"Hey!" the guy next to him called again as he sifted through the piles of dollar bills. "I put a twenty down instead of a ten. I want it back."

"No, you didn't," Vyr said in the cool voice that said he was pissed and trying not to show it. "I watched you. You put a five down."

"Fuck you, no I didn't. I want my twenty back."

Candace bent down and locked eyes on Torren. He could see the exact moment the flip got switched back because her eyes went from vacant to locked and focused on him. "Torren?" she asked in a sweet, clear-as-a-bell voice. "What are you doing here?"

"Clearly not paying like I did," the man said, sifting through the money frantically.

"If you take a single bill from that stage, I'm going to kick your ass," Torren warned.

"Fuck you."

"Jerry, I'm not doing this again," Candace said, scooping the money toward her.

Jerry slapped his hand on a twenty and scrambled to yank it out from under Candace's hand.

"Stop!" Candace yelled. "Carl! Shit, where is he?" she asked, looking around frantically.

When Jerry grabbed her wrist, Torren was good and done. The gorilla stayed put thanks to Vyr's order, but he was on Jerry so fast the sleazeball didn't even know what hit him. Torren lifted him off the ground by his throat. "The lady has a rule, asshole. No touching. And no stealing money. She's working, not you. Now fuck off before I pop your head off your neck." Torren offered him an empty smile and released the choking, red-faced man.

Jerry hit the floor like a sack of stones and then scrambled backward, coughing hard. Torren had been so tempted to collapse that fragile little human trachea, but he'd been a good monkey and let the idiot survive.

A deep, rumbling growl vibrated up his throat as his silverback practically hummed with satisfaction. "Who's next?" Torren taunted the others who were now crowding around. "Who else wants to break the rules? Hmm? No one? That's what I fuckin' thought. Candace?"

"Yes?" she asked.

When he turned, she was standing with her legs locked, staring with wide, inhumanly gold eyes at him. "You go on and do what you want. I'll collect your money and clear the stage for the next dance. You need anything?"

Stunned, Candace scanned the crowd and a small, wicked smile took her lips. "Yeah. A drink."

God, her grin was boner-inducing. He matched it and asked, "What do you drink?"

"Guess."

Oh, kitty wanted to play. "Okay, I'll bring it to you."

"Good. I'll be in the private room, waiting."

"What the hell?" Jerry squawked as the other men muttered under their breaths with the same sentiments. "This guy has been in here one time. He ain't a loyal customer like the rest of us!"

Candace wasn't listening, though. She was marching that firm little ass away and exiting stage left. And when she cast one last glance at Torren, she flashed him the sexiest come-hither smile that had ever graced a woman's lips. Fuck, she was gorgeous. All done up in her glitter and big hair and false eyelashes or dressed down and natural like earlier at the mansion, this girl had all his attention, and his silverback's attention, too. He'd felt like a rutting animal since the first moment he saw her out the window.

Torren gathered the money and stacked it quick. He would sort it out later like he did with his fight money, but for now, he shoved that pile into his back pocket and sauntered toward the bar.

"What happened?" a thin-haired, lanky man in his mid-forties asked as he came from the back. Probably Carl who, by the way, sucked at his job because Candace had called out for help, and where the hell was he?

"I took care of it," Torren gritted out as he passed.

He ordered them both a double vodka and sprite with lime because Candace was a good mix of soft and hard. She wasn't straight whiskey, but she wasn't tequila and margarita mix either.

Drinks in hand, Torren made his way to the back and gave Vyr a dirty look for having a stupid smirk on his dumb face like he owned a crystal ball and knew everything in the world. He might be his best friend, but Vyr was too cocky for his own good.

At least Nox wasn't here to annoy him. Least best friend.

Torren shoved the door open to find Candace standing on the back of a black leather couch, sticking duct tape over a camera lens up in the corner. "There's no volume on it," she explained.

"Carl won't be mad that you blocked his view?" That guy was probably a perv.

"Carl has enough to deal with because I just called him on that little phone and told him I'm not doing my last dance so I can give you a private show. I told him you have tons of mullah." Candace smiled brightly and held out her hand.

With an amused chuckle, Torren handed her the stack of money she'd earned.

"I'm rich," she whispered, waggling her dark, delicately arched eyebrows.

Torren bit his bottom lip and slid his hands to her waist. She was on her knees on the couch. So. Fucking. Sexy.

"I'm not gonna dance for you for money," she murmured, her eyes going serious.

"I would never ask you to."

She searched his eyes and ran her hands up his abs. God, her touch felt so good. She didn't stop until her open palms rested on his chest. Slowly, Torren leaned down but hesitated right before he kissed her. He gave her the option of backing out, but she held her ground. One more second, and he pressed his lips gently to hers.

They held just like that for a couple moments, and then she parted her lips for him and let him brush his tongue inside her mouth. Damn, she tasted so good. He didn't want to push, but he sure as hell didn't want this to stop either. She was doing something strange to him. Every time he dipped his tongue onto hers, she relaxed a little more against him, and his gorilla grew more and more still until he didn't feel like he existed at all. It was just Torren and Candace. A man and woman. A boy and girl. Two people who were building the beginnings of…something. She was terrifying and interesting and a gorgeous distraction from the suck.

Candace pecked him once, twice, nipped his lip, and then stunned him when she slipped her arms around his neck and rested her cheek against his in a hug. A hug? When was the last time he hugged a girl? But he didn't hate it. She was so small in his arms, he felt like a giant. Felt protective of her. Felt like the beast to her beauty. His heart was pounding so hard. Could she feel it against her chest? Could she hear it?

Fuck, what was she doing now? Candace rubbed her soft cheek against his beard, making a scratching sound that rivaled the softest purr in her throat.

"You're getting stripper glitter on me," he murmured.

"Good." She eased back and switched cheeks. "Guess what I did?"

"Hmmmm?" he rumbled, damn near in a trance from whatever she was doing to his body.

"I rigged up the television with a movie."

With a frown, Torren leaned back to look in her eyes. They were gold, and he bet she was a beauty in her animal form. Pretty kitty. "Like a porn?"

"No!" she said with a laugh. "Don't be a gross boy. I found a comedy. This is date number two." She looked and smelled happy, eyes bright as she stared up at him, waiting for a response.

This girl was more interesting by the second. Torren told her, "You have a lot more to you than I thought you would."

"What do you mean?"

"I mean you're a bad girl in the ways I like, but then you surprise me because you're a good girl, too. Perfect balance and so damn interesting. You make me want to watch you."

"Like a stalker?"

"Don't give HavoK any ideas. No, I mean you make me want to figure you out."

"You mean you want to study me."

"No. Study is the wrong word."

"What's the right word?"

"There's no single right word. You make me want to be around you so I can figure out your secrets. You make me want to be around you so I can feel…"

"Feel what?" she murmured, stroking the hair at the back of his head with gentle fingers.

"Maybe just feel anything. Confusing woman. I'm supposed to be numb right now. I'm supposed to stay steady, and then you came in, and sometimes I want to test myself and see if I can stay steady around you."

"Maybe you can."

"Until our first fight. Until you do something that upsets me."

"Like what?"

"Like leaving. You'll get me hooked, won't you, Wildcat? Get me hooked and then leave, and I'll spiral so hard I won't get to make it to my sister's surgery. You're dangerous to a man like me."

"And you're dangerous to a girl like me."

"Good girl," he said. "Now you're getting it. I'm not a safe man to be friends with."

"I don't mean like that."

Baffled, Torren shook his head slightly.

He was about to ask how he was a danger to her if she didn't mean physically, but she picked up a remote off the couch cushion and turned the TV on behind them. Then plopped back against the leather cushion and slapped the seat beside her. "Come here, Prince Kong HavoK Danger Monkey. I stole us a bag of Skittles to share from Carl's candy stash. I'm greedy though and like the reds, but dislike the yellows, so guess what you're getting?"

Torren chuckled and sank onto the couch beside her. "I don't mind the yellows." Actually, they were his least favorite, but his voice had come out completely honest. Huh. Really, he just wanted her to be happy and comfortable, and he would've picked the reds out of five bags of Skittles just to make a whole bag of them for her.

"Watch this," Candace said with an overly bright grin. She clapped twice, and the lights dimmed.

"Gross," he said with a laugh as he imagined all the gyrating that had happened in this room at the dimming of the clap lights.

"Super gross, but I kind of want that in my house someday."

The beginning credits were playing on the television, but Torren didn't even know what they were watching because his attention was taken by Candace. "Do you live in a house now?"

"Tiiiiiny apartment a few blocks away." She scrunched up her cute little nose. "It has roaches when it's hot."

"I can get rid of them. I'll spray them."

Her face went comically blank. "Really?"

"Yeah, really. It's easy. I'll probably have to come out and do it a few times, but I'll get rid of your pest problem."

"Huh." She stared at the television for a few seconds and then asked again in a higher pitch, "Really?"

"It's not a big deal. Any friend would do it for you."

"Can I tell you something?"

"Tell me anything. No judgement. I'm a bigger devil than you."

Candace hesitated, then laid back on the couch, rested her head on the armrest, and draped her bare legs across his lap. Now he was damn-near purring like a cat. He dragged his fingertips down her smooth thigh and rested his hand on her bent knee. "Did you change your mind?"

"No, I'm just thinking if I want to tell you or not. I don't talk about this stuff. Not with anyone."

"Well, the benefit of having a crazy

acquaintance who is about to be put down is your secrets will go to a grave, and quick."

"Don't ever talk like that," she said, her eyes blazing a lighter gold. "Even if that's what you think will happen, don't talk about it."

"So we'll pretend this can go on forever?"

"Yes. And now I have decided I will tell you, because you of all people should hear."

"Okay. I'm ready."

"I dance to pay off my dad's medical bills. He was an older shifter when he had me. He got sick."

"What kind of sick?" Shifters didn't get sick often, but they also weren't supposed to be born deaf, and Genevieve, his sister, had been.

"It was a degenerative disease. The doctors couldn't figure it out. It took his muscles and bones over time and was very painful. He was eighty pounds soaking wet when he died last year. He was in hospice for seven months, and it was expensive. I took care of him with a nurse. We took shifts, and to pay her and the medical bills, I started dancing at nights because what else could I do here? What could I do with my skillset that would bring me cash everyday? When I needed to pay a bill fast, I just picked up double shifts at Jem's. Before he got sick, I used to come here to spend the summers with him and then go back to my life in New York. I wanted to be a dancer. A real dancer. I auditioned for fancy schools, but even if I had gotten in, we couldn't afford them. So I worked at this bar, doing these shows. Dancing with other girls. I choreographed everything for them, and when I had enough money saved up, I bought this little rundown studio, and I taught dance classes to kids. I was happy, except I missed my dad. And then he got sick, and I came home. Things got worse, and I sold the studio to pay some of his bills. You know from your sister shifters don't get health insurance. And then he passed away, and I still had all these loans under my name, so I'm just trying to tread water until I can get everything paid."

"So you're stuck?"

Candace's eyes held phantoms as she nodded once. "Stuck like I've been buried alive. Most days

I feel buried. So, look at me now. A trained dancer who had achieved her dream, owned a studio, found happiness, and now I'm here, scooping dollar bills off the ground in a negligee and 'stripper glitter.'"

"Fuck," Torren murmured, feeling sick to his stomach. He wished with everything he had that he could yank her out of here and fix her life. Make it better. Make it happier. Make it brighter before she got crushed by the weight of the world. "Come here." He held out his arm and waited while she sat up and snuggled against his ribs. God, she felt like she belonged there, like she'd been made to fit right against him. There was nothing he could say to make it better, so he propped his feet up on the small table in front of them and leaned back. With a sigh, he rested his cheek on the top of her head. And after a few minutes, he said, "I'm gonna take you somewhere tonight."

"On a date?"

"No," he murmured. "You won't like this, but you'll watch it and you'll witness it, and you won't feel so alone. Okay?"

She looked up with those pretty tiger eyes and clutched his T-shirt right over his pounding heart. "You gonna show me your demon's now?"

He nodded. He'd never invited anyone to watch what he was about to do.

"Which demon?"

"I'm going to show you HavoK." Torren pulled her tighter against him. "And then I'm going to ask you not to run."

EIGHT

The old sawmill looked downright creepy at night.

Torren slid his hand over her thigh as he eased his black Camaro into a dirt parking lot. His headlights arced across the front of the old, dilapidated building. The rusted sign on the front read Foxburg Mill, but someone had marked that out with spray paint and written HavoK. A little skull was painted beside it, similar to the logo on the T-shirt he was wearing right now.

"Did you do that?" she asked, pointing to the sign as he pulled to a stop.

"Nope. Vyr did. And Nox drew the dick."

She squinted and, yep, there was a little cherry-red penis spray-painted underneath the skull. She giggled. Of course, Nox did that. "Can I ask you something?"

Torren squeezed her leg comfortably and rolled his head on the rest to look at her. His eyes glowed green, and he smelled only of silverback, nothing like a man. But he was still here in his human skin, and he didn't look worried about Changing in his car. "Shoot."

"I can't get this out of my head. Nevada...when I saw her at Vyr's mansion, she was so different from the mouse I talked to in the library. Why?"

"Because she's ours, and we're hers," he answered simply.

It gave her chills. She would do just about anything to have something like that. To not feel like this iceberg out in the middle of a frigid sea, surviving on her own. "I like your crew."

"They're a disaster. Worst crew in the world. We're all fuck-ups."

"But for someone looking in from the outside?

Whatever you doing? It works. Maybe you're fuck-ups individually, but together? You've got the biggest, baddest alpha in the entire world. And there are only three of you propping him up—you, Nox, and Nevada. Vyr is dangerous, but you live with him like you aren't afraid of his fire. You speak to him like you aren't afraid of him being a man-eater. You went after him yesterday, for me, like you weren't afraid of his wrath at all." She intertwined her fingers with his. "I think the Red Dragon needs that. I think he needs you guys to keep him steady."

Torren cut the engine. "When I was a kid, my dad took me to Damon Daye's mansion. He'd summoned me. Vyr was lonely and acting out, and none of the other kids could handle his dragon. He couldn't control his Changes, and he—burned—everything. And everyone. Anyone who got in the path of his fire got hurt, and he couldn't do anything about it. He was seven when I was brought in. Damon had been watching me. He saw how dominant I was, saw me fighting my way through school, saw me loyal to no one, but yearning to be part of something. Beaston, this seer in the Gray Backs, told Damon to put me in the path of Vyr's fire and *watch* what happened. We played for two days before I saw the Red dragon. He was much smaller. Baby dragon. I was an adolescent gorilla but big for my age. He burned me one time. Grazed my arm with his fire, and I charged. I was pissed, but more than that, I was worried because I'd seen his eyes when he blasted that stream of fire at me. He didn't want to do it. I could see him trying to stop himself. I jumped into the air and, with my arms around his wings, slammed us both back down to earth. And while he struggled and clicked his firestarter like he would light me up again, I talked in my gorilla form for the first time. It was out of desperation. I was a kid, but I wanted to save us both. I screamed at him to, 'Stop or you'll hurt me! You'll hurt me, and I'll never be your friend again. I won't be your friend, Vyr. I won't!' And he swallowed that fire. It hurt him, but he swallowed it and went still. And since then, he hasn't ever burned me. Oh, he'll light everyone else up, but not me. He's dangerous and out of control, but I'm his keeper. He's gonna mess up someday. He's gonna mess up in a way he can't come back from, and he'll take me with him. I accepted that the day I stopped him from burning me. Age seven, and I pledged fealty to the Red Dragon. Dragons tend to get loyal to someone. Damon has Mason. They become loyal to a friend until they find a mate. Seven years old, and he picked me as his friend, and I picked him back. We're both going to Hell, Candace. Don't think we're salvageable because we aren't. Nox isn't either. We're all going to Hell, but we're going together. You like the crew, but we're on a fast train headed for fire. It scares me to reach out and pull you onto it. You would be better off picking anyone else to be around."

"Who else would match me?" she asked quietly. "Who, Torren? I hopped that train way before I met you. Hell doesn't scare me anymore."

A green Mustang parked beside them, and Torren blew out a sharp breath. "We'll see about that."

"Who is that?" she asked, confused.

"That's my fight. HavoK has to do this. If he fights regularly, he lets me keep a little bit of control. I'm light on cash, so lately I've been setting up fights for money. Wait there," he murmured as he pushed open his door.

She thought he wanted to conduct the business part of this fight without her, but he shocked her when he ignored the two giants getting out of the Mustang and opened her door instead.

"You just opened my door for me," she said low, shocked to her bones.

"You're a queen, Candace. Never think you're anything less." Those words were beautiful coming from a man like Torren. He stood there, tall and strong, his calloused, tattooed hand held out for her, his blazing inhuman eyes the color of glowing moss, his jaw clenched, and his face stern as if he was already focused on this fight. He was about to get hurt, but he was making sure she didn't slip on her way out of his car.

And for the first time in maybe ever, out in the

dirty parking lot of a fight shack, she actually felt like a queen—because of Torren.

When she slipped her hand against his, there was that sharp pain in her chest again. The one that kept happening. The one that had happened when she told him about her dad earlier in the private room and he'd pulled her against him and made her feel instantly better. Sharp pain in her chest, then a numbing sensation. Torren was a drug, and she had a feeling this was the moment. She could quit this drug now, or give into the addiction and fall head first into the fire with Torren.

Quit or stay.

Quit or stay.

Quit and avoid the Hell he was headed for, or stay and dig her heels in and get loyal, have his back no matter what, watch him get hurt, watch him fight, watch him struggle with his animal, watch his brokenness, watch him be the keeper of the Red Dragon, watch the consequences of his fealty.

Chills rippling up her arm, she gripped his hand and allowed him to pull her out of his car.

She wasn't some fair-weather friend, and she sure as hell wasn't a runner.

Candace was staying.

She was in this, no matter what.

Torren pulled her against him and kissed her quick. It was two fast dips of his tongue into her mouth and a nip to her bottom lip that left her panting and needy. As he pulled away, he slid something into her hand, and when she looked down, it was a stack of twenty-dollar bills. He held her gaze for a moment more before he turned toward the two men standing in front of the Mustang.

"Which one of you?" Torren asked.

"Me," the tank of a man in front said. "I'm Colt Caraway." He waited a few seconds with his eyebrows lifted like Torren should know the name. He had burred hair and scars down one side of his face. Teeth marks from the looks of it. A lot of them. He reeked of dominance. His eyes were glowing blue as he dragged his attention down her body and back up. "Which one of you?" he asked with a smirk.

"She's mine," Torren said coolly. He stretched his neck, popping it, one way and then the other. "You'll be mine, too."

"We'll see, HavoK. You can't go undefeated forever, you know. You ain't invincible. Someday, someone is gonna come along and knock you on your ass. Maybe today is that day. Maybe I'm supposed to be the new Kong."

Torren was already walking toward the sawmill though, peeling off his shirt as he went. His giant birthmark was stark against his pale skin in the moonlight. That was the best "fuck you" he could've given Colt, and Candace pursed her lips against a smile.

A snarl rippled up the man's throat, and he followed Torren across the parking lot and inside.

"I'm Dax. Are you HavoK's manager?" the other man asked. He was shorter, but still built like a Mack truck. His eyes were softer, but he still smelled of fur.

"No. I'm just a witness," she murmured.

He gestured to the money in her hand. "Not anymore, little girl."

"Careful with that term," she popped off, barely containing the hiss in her throat. She hated to be put beneath people. "Where's his money?"

"You need to see it?" Dax asked, looking irritated.

"Did I stutter? I don't know you, and I sure as fuck don't know him. You want this fight? Show me his money, and we can let those boys loose. HavoK won't start without me in there." She hoped.

"Mmmm," Dax rumbled. Definitely a silverback shifter. He waited a few too many seconds to be polite, looking down his nose at her, and then he pulled a wad of rolled cash out of his back pocket. "You want to count it, too?"

She could really use less of his sarcasm. Already she wanted to let her tiger have him.

"Ha, I think if you shorted us, the *real* Kong would rip your throat out. I don't trust you, but I think you like survival. Let's go."

"What are you?" he asked from behind her as

she led him to the sawmill.

She turned to face him but didn't stop walking. He was holding up his phone like he was taking video. Hands out, she said, "I'm just a little girl." Fucker.

"I think you're his manager. You just don't know it yet. What's your name?"

She was smart enough not to give away anything on video. Candace turned back around and reached for the splintered door handle. "Maybe I'm the real HavoK." He was only getting the dead voice from her because he was a part of what was about to get Torren hurt.

Inside, a trio of hanging lightbulbs lit up the sawmill with a dim glow. It was an enormous room with stairs against the back wall leading to an office on the second floor with a massive, broken picture window that separated it from the rest of the mill. The walls were made of old logs, gone gray and warped with age. The floor was covered in piles of saw dust. Old machines with rusted blades and saws lined the perimeter of the room. There were deep divots in the floors as though the saws had been shoved to their resting places by force. It smelled of oil and sawdust, dominance, fur...blood. Lots of blood.

The clearing in the center of the room was stained dark. She had to force the snarl in her throat to stay quiet. Her big cat was getting riled up...bloodlust maybe...or maybe she was feeling protective. How much of this was Torren's blood? God, he had to do this, right? To keep steady? To keep his animal from going insane, he had to bleed? She wanted to retch.

Candace paused at the edge of the makeshift ring where Dax took a stand beside her. Annoying. She wished he would go over there, on the other side, with his fighter.

Across the room, Colt was stripping down, attention on Torren, who was sitting on a rickety old bench against the wall, elbows resting on his knees, hands clenched, teeth gritted. He lifted his roiling gaze to her. *Everything okay?* his eyes seemed to ask. She nodded once.

"Colt needs this win," Dax said. "He needs a family group. Do you know what Torren has done to the gorillas?"

She didn't answer. She didn't want him to know how little she knew about Torren's culture.

"He probably wouldn't have told you how he betrayed our people, huh? No one wants to admit when they're the downfall of an entire shifter race. His betrayal started with his father and continued with him."

"There are two sides to every story," she gritted out, eyes on Torren as he shucked his pants, eyes on the bloody floor. He was masculinity and power in just his briefs, every muscle flexed.

"True. So listen to the other side. The Kong should run our people. He should be making the next generation. He should be heading up the biggest family group of females. It's an easy life. Be born with the mark, grow dominant, have all the sex you want. Be. King. His father shunned his duty, and Torren did, too. At eighteen, he was offered the throne, and what did he do? Denied it, threw our people into chaos looking for a new Kong. There isn't one, though. The tradition of the Kong was wrecked by Torren's father and destroyed completely by Torren. And then he did something unforgiveable. When our people wanted vengeance against Red Havoc, he went to war against us—his own people."

"You went after the crew with his sister in it. What did you expect to happen?"

"He betrayed all of his people for one female."

Dax's voice was appalled, and Candace slid him a dirty glare. "*Your* people are not his people. He didn't betray his people. You went after his people and you got burned. Literally. Your bad. Also, this makes me think gorillas are super-messed up. The fact that you can't see a reason for him protecting his own sister? I don't blame Torren for not wanting to *breed* a bunch of females. I don't blame him for giving two middle fingers to that poisoned throne either." She gave her attention back to Torren just as his monster silverback ripped out of him and landed with his giant fists on the floorboard, cracking the wooden planks underneath. "He wasn't ever meant to be king of a fucked-up people. He was meant to be this. He was meant to be HavoK." He was meant to keep the world safe from Vyr. He was meant to live his life on his terms. Nothing this gorilla said was going to change what she saw—the real Torren.

Torren and Colt stood on their hind legs and beat their chests. The loud drum of it filled the room, and Candace covered her sensitive ears. The silverbacks charged and hit each other with the force of a head-on collision.

As they slammed their fists against each other in a flurry of violence, Dax began to pace and yell at his fighter. Colt spun out of Torren's grip and scrambled for the wall, Torren right on his heels. The two scaled the wall like it was nothing. Candace couldn't even tell where they'd found purchase before they were up in the rafters.

Torren was so much bigger than he'd looked in the video she'd watched, the one where he'd gone to battle and Vyr had burned Covington. Seeing him in real life was eye-opening. He was bigger than wild gorillas. He was eight hundred pounds, at least, of pure muscle and power. Massive front arms and a sloping back. She followed the chase as the man next to her yelled for Colt to, "Stop playing defense and fight!" He was agitated, passing tighter now, growling. Shit.

"Settle," she warned him.

"Don't tell me what to do, bitch."

Oh, she wanted to rip his throat out, but Torren didn't need the distraction. Candace clenched her hands against the urge to Change. *Come on, Torren. End this quick.*

"Fight, Colt!! Fight or I'll finish this! Don't let this asshole shame you. Lock him up!"

Candace blew out a breath, half her attention on the fight happening thirty feet above them, half on the man who was snarling louder beside her. When he gritted his teeth, his canines were too long.

"There is no money happening for you if you go two on one against him," she warned. "Seriously. Settle."

A gorilla fell from the rafters, and for a horrifying second, she thought it was Torren. But a moment later, Torren landed on all fours right beside him, buckling the flooring beneath his massive knuckles with a deafening crash. He pulled himself easily out of the rubble and went to blows with Colt. Their gorillas were similar sizes, but Torren kept the upper hand, didn't even look like he was trying.

The man beside her gritted his teeth and let off a bellow. With a smattering of pops, his silverback broke out of him.

Crap, crap, crap!

He charged Torren, and now the shit had officially hit the fan.

"Torren!" she screamed.

He jerked his attention over his shoulder just in time to catch Dax's weight full on his back.

She'd always been proud of her control over her animal, but that went out the window now. *Mine. He's fucking mine. Mine, mine, mine! Roaaaar*! Her body broke, and oh it hurt for the instant it took.

Bones broke, muscles snapped, teeth elongated, claws pierced her paws.

Colt was back in the fight now, wailing on Torren as he went to battle with Dax. Two massive gorillas on one, but Torren was a beast. He didn't show any pain under the blows. He didn't even flinch when Dax sank his teeth into his shoulder blade and ripped backward to inflict maximum damage. He just kept fighting, ripped Dax's face off him as he twisted, eyes now focused on Colt. The shift between his fights with each were smooth and lightning fast.

Dax was hanging off his back while Torren was still engaged with Colt. There was no honor in Dax fighting two on one and going after an exposed back, so Candace bolted for him and pounced, claws out. She latched onto his ribs, surprised at how thick his skin was. It was hard to find purchase with her claws, but she sank her teeth into his side as hard as she could—so hard her jaw hurt.

Dax roared and released Torren, and then with a big, meaty hand, he reached over his shoulder, grabbed her by the scruff of the neck, and yanked her off him. She was airborne and then hit the wall.

Vyr. Vyr! Vyr can you hear me? she screamed in her mind. *Torren needs you!*

She didn't know what made her do that. Perhaps it was the instant and intense pain of crashing through the wall, or the desperation she felt seeing two gorillas at war with the man she cared about.

Vyr terrified her, but he loved Torren and she was no match for silverbacks.

Ignoring her bruised side, Candace forced herself up onto all fours. Her ribs were probably cracked. Limping, she ran back to the fight. It smelled like blood. The overpowering scent of iron made her dizzy. Torren was on Dax now, but Colt was taking advantage of his exposed neck. He could kill him like this! She attacked Colt and just went vicious. Biting, clawing, she pulled him away from the fight and distracted him enough for Torren to focus on Dax. She was slammed to the ground, and time slowed. Eyes blazing like blue fire, Colt lifted his arm into the air and slammed it down toward her face. And right before he made contact, he was ripped backward through the wall of the sawmill, wood planks blasting out with him.

Candace winced as splinters from the exploding wall rained over her. What the hell?

When she turned, Torren was standing over her defensively, and Dax was ripping an old rusted blade from one of the machines. He swung it at Torren's throat, but Torren stood on his hind legs and ducked easily out of the way of the jagged, razor-sharp teeth.

Vyr, Vyr, Vyr. Vyr!

She roared and stalked Dax. Colt was still outside, and she couldn't even hear him anymore. All she could hear were the grunts and snarls from the warring gorillas facing off. She crouched beside Torren and pulled her lips back from her teeth with a long, warning hiss. *Swing that fuckin' blade one more time, and I'm gonna light you up.*

Dax hesitated at a rumbling noise, and it took her a moment to place the strange sound. It was getting louder and louder, and suddenly, Torren wrapped his arm around her middle and spun her out of the way. A horrific crash sounded and then splintering wood was everywhere. Torren was moving so fast she couldn't catch her breath, and in a matter of moments, she was up in the rafters with him. Below them, the Mustang had crashed through the wall of the sawmill. Dax was searching for something in the rubble. He picked up his cell phone just as Torren let go of the rafter and landed gracefully, saving Candace from the impact.

With grim determination written all over his face, Dax yanked the passenger door open and shoved his giant gorilla ass into the tiny car. With his arm and head hanging out the window, Dax, the gorilla, shoved his meaty middle finger into the air as Colt zoomed backward out of the hole he'd made. The memory of this would probably be funny tomorrow, but right now, she mostly wanted to kill them and set their car on fire.

"That went well," Torren said sarcastically in that snarling, inhuman voice of his. He was staring at the hole with an exhausted expression. His arm was shredded and dripping crimson on the floorboards.

More stains on this place.

More mess.

More HavoK.

He arched his gaze down to her. "You scared yet, Wildcat?"

She was bruised, out of breath, limping, shocked, angry, and her eyes were now open to what a power-house Torren was.

But scared of this life she was melting into?

She hissed at him.

Hell no.

NINE

Torren had bolted.

That was the only word she could think of when he asked her to stay where she was in that sexy, snarly voice of his. Stay while he gracefully glided on all fours toward a dilapidated staircase. He didn't take the stairs like a human, nope. He scaled the side of it, pulling himself up and up until he slipped over the ledge and made his way into the office on the second level. The big window was cracked, but she could still see his rampage and hear the deafening crash as he threw something against the wall.

He was king. She was going to dig in and do as

much research about gorilla shifters as possible, but he'd gone to war with two massive silverbacks tonight and held his own. And then he'd shelved his rage—for her. But now he was losing it up there.

Her heart ached for him.

Inhaling deep, she closed her eyes and tucked her tiger back inside her. The clothes she'd worn would be shredded and useless, even if she could find them under the pile of rubble. She still tried, rummaging around for at least a shirt, but stopped when she found the two wads of cash. Cash he'd fought for. Cash he would give to his sister so she could hear.

There was another deafening crash above. He'd asked her to stay down here so she wouldn't have to witness the rage that took the animal after a fight gone bad, but it was important that she see it.

Slowly, she made her way up the stairs, and at the top, she stared sadly at a big dent in the middle of the metal door. She put her fist in it. It was much bigger than her own knuckles—that of a silverback fist.

Pain. This was a man full of pain, and stuck in a life he couldn't escape. Being king wasn't all it was cracked up to be when the crown didn't fit the man.

Candace pushed open the door and stepped inside. She hesitated. There had been a desk, but it was in splinters. There were holes in the walls and broken chairs, a broken bookshelf. The only thing left untouched was a charcoal gray couch where Torren sat, face in his battered, tattooed hands. He was human again, and his black hair stood up in spikes as though he'd ran his hands through it roughly. He was still puffed up, every muscle in his body tensed.

"I don't want you to see me like this. Afterward…it's hard."

"Because of guilt?"

"Most of the time," he rumbled, not removing his face from his hands. "Tonight, it's different."

After the span of a few heartbeats, Candace made her way to him, pushed his shoulders back, and straddled his lap. She cupped his cheeks and searched his blazing green eyes. "Tell me."

Torren was pale, and streams of drying blood ran down his chest from a bite at the base of his neck that was already closed, and well on its way to healing. Powerhouse. Powerful. Magic. The new Kong would be damn near invincible if he took his place at the head of the gorillas.

"You Changed," he murmured, slipping his giant hands to her bare hips. He gripped her hard and clenched his teeth. "You Changed to defend me, and you were so fucking beautiful. Fearless. I got to see you for the first time. Tigress. Badass. Tiiiiny stripes. All orange and white, eyes blazing with the promise of vengeance for those gorillas. Why?"

"I told Dax to settle. That he couldn't go two gorillas on one. He didn't listen, and I wasn't going to watch you get shredded."

"You wouldn't, would you? You're a ride-or-die girl, aren't you, Candace?"

She nodded once.

"Fuck." Torren gave his attention to the side, but she pulled his face back to her.

"You pulled Colt off me before he got to my face. You protected me, too. You're a ride-or-die too, aren't you, HavoK?"

He smirked and let off a single humorless laugh. "I think you knew that before you saw me defend you. Because of Vyr."

"Vyr, and now me. You gonna make me safe, Torren?"

"You're so fucking safe around me, it's ridiculous. Anyone who messes with you? They're in trouble. I won't have much control over what I do to them."

She rolled her eyes closed at that oath. "I haven't felt safe since my dad died. I've been on my own, in this world I didn't prepare for."

"The club?"

"Yes. I was a good girl, and now I'm not."

"Fuck that noise. You're good enough, Candace. If you were your old self, you wouldn't be here, taming a riled-up silverback shifter in an old sawmill. You wouldn't have gone teeth and claws first after a dominant shifter just to protect a wreck like me. You wouldn't have looked twice at me."

"You're wrong."

"I'm not. I wouldn't have let you. I think what you've been through has toughened you up. It's conditioned you to match me. I wasn't sure, but I think after tonight, you won't be walking behind me or in front of me. You'll be perfectly comfortable right beside me. Won't you?"

She ran her nails down the sides of his head and smiled when he was the one who rolled his eyes closed and made a satisfied rumbling sound deep in his throat. "Bad Boy from Damon's Mountains. Are you saying we match?"

"Bad Girl from Vyr's Mountains. I think the person you are now is maybe the person I need." His grip tightened on her waist, and he dragged her forward onto his hard erection. "Any softer, and I would be too scared to draw you into my life. Any harder, and you couldn't tame the monster inside of me. And that's what you're doing…right? That's why I'm Changed back now and settled. Why I'm not beating myself up, wondering why I can't be less fucked-up like other shifters. It's why tonight is easy. Why I feel fine being just who I am."

"If you weren't this. If you weren't HavoK, I don't think I could feel safe like I need to. I've chased every boy away because they made me feel like I needed to pretend to be normal, and good. You're different. I don't need money, Torren. I can take care of myself. My love language doesn't include lavish presents. It's feeling safe with someone, and comfortable being in my own skin. It's having someone accept me, even the gritty parts."

A slow smile stretched Torren's lips. "I understand. I'm the same."

"Date number three."

Torren's slow smile was wicked and understanding. "One. Dinner with my crew."

"Two," she played along. "You saw me at my worst in the club, and then a movie and cuddling in the private room. Maybe that isn't what some people would call a date, but we're different. And I used to be ashamed of being different, but for some reason, with you, I'm proud to be what I am. Because you're like me and I don't have to apologize."

"Mmmm," he murmured low, looking proud. "Date number three. The fight. You saw me at my worst. You didn't run like I was afraid you would."

"I'm not a runner. Never was." She rolled her hips against his, and he groaned and dug his fingers into her waist. He rocked, meeting her movement. Sexy. Monster.

"I'll make a promise to you, okay?" she whispered.

Torren leaned up and kissed her, sucked her lip and released her. "Okay. Promises."

"I'll come to every fight. I'll have your back. I'll handle the money. I know people. I have connections through the club. I can set up fights when you need them. I'll print my own HavoK T-shirt, for me. Pink logo on a black shirt, and I'll wear it proudly. I'll advertise for your fights and make sure they're as organized as they can be. I'll keep what happened tonight from happening again.

I'll make fair fights. I'll be your teammate and make sure you never do this alone. Because I see you, Torren. I hate that you have to do this. I hate the scent of your blood. Hate that the floorboards downstairs are stained because of your pain. But what good will it do if I ask you to stop? I understand now that I've seen you fight. You telling me is one thing, but seeing it is different. To hold your ground and stay off that gorilla throne you have to do this, don't you? You have to fight to keep HavoK stable. To keep sane, so you can continue the work you do protecting Vyr from the world, and the world from Vyr."

Torren swallowed hard and murmured, "I think you see me very well."

"Okay. Then I accept you, Torren. All of it. I accept the gritty parts and the soft parts. I accept the protective parts, the loyal parts, and I accept the things you have to do as a man to stay steady. You're perfect to me." Her eyes burned because his chest was heaving and he looked so emotional. "I. Accept. You. I'm not running. I'm here. I'm right here."

Torren was shaking now. He ripped his gaze away from hers and then back. "My turn. When you dance, I'll be your bodyguard. You have bills to pay, you got in a hole, you have your dad's medical stuff to take care of, and I'm not asking you to quit what you're doing just to make me comfortable. You aren't telling me to quit fighting, so I accept you back. I'll be quiet. I'll talk to Carl about hiring me as security, and if he doesn't, I'll still show up every night and make sure you're safe. Make sure you always feel safe. Make sure no one touches you. I'll collect your money after you dance because you shouldn't be on your knees doing that. You're a fucking queen, Candace. If I ever see your crown slipping, I'll always straighten it back." Torren swallowed hard, his Adam's apple dipping into his thick, tattooed neck. "You're perfect to me." He kissed her gently, then eased back by an inch and whispered. "I. Accept. You."

Chills rippled up her body, and inside she went as warm as magma. It was a strange sensation, but the best feeling she'd ever had.

She didn't have to be ashamed. She didn't have to be anyone other than herself with this man. They were both flawed, but lucky for them, both of their demons played well together. And that's what finding a mate was, right? It was being able to be real with a person. It was giving two middle fingers to that instinct to hide. It was stepping into the light, flaws and all, and staring that man in the eyes and daring him to leave, knowing he wouldn't. She wasn't too much for him, and he wasn't too much for her.

She'd never felt such a sense of belonging than she did right here, in this moment.

He pulled her close, their bare chests creating warmth between them. He slid his hand up her spine to the back of her neck and gripped it, hugged her tight.

With a happy purr, she nuzzled her face to the uninjured side of his neck. And on a whim, she nipped him. Just a hint of teeth, and then she released his throat. *My big silverback. My man.*

Torren yanked her back, and then his lips crashed onto hers. His hips went graceful, rolling his hard dick against her. She was already wet and prepped for him, so three more pumps, and she was done with playing. Candace lifted slightly, gripped his thick shaft, and slid over him slowly, watching his focus on her intensify as she did.

"Fuuuuck," Torren rumbled, one hand hard on her hip, guiding her, and one hand gripping the back of her hair.

When he bucked and went deep on the next stroke, Candace was already gone. She took all of him so that he hit her clit just right. The sharp pain was back in her chest, but just for a moment, and then it was that warm sensation. Ecstasy. She rocked faster, kept him deep, teased him as his muscles twitched. He pulled her closer, and he moved against her, hips meeting hers time after time.

He felt so fucking good inside of her. Perfect. Like everything. He really was her match.

Needy sounds escaped her throat every time he

bumped that right spot. Torren was being gentle. Oh, she was smashed against him, but he was pure power and could crush her. He was staying in control, being just rough enough to keep it fun.

"Oh, God, Oh, God, Candace!" he gritted out.

And then suddenly, she was flipped to her back on the couch, and Torren was even deeper, thrusting so hard, so fast, ramming her upward until her head was at the arm rest. Holy shit, he was beautiful. Muscles rippling above her, abs flexing against her stomach as he stroked into her. Big rutting beast of a man losing control over her. Faster, faster, deeper, and the sounds in his throat said he was close with her.

He grabbed her hand and slammed it on the armrest above her head, pinning her in a submissive position, but she liked it. She snarled and arched her back as her body exploded around him. Torren yelled out as his dick throbbed hard inside of her, matching her release. It was so intense she closed her eyes and gripped his hand as hard as she could.

And then there was his rough beard against her

neck. One second of that, and then there was pain, a sharp, driving ache at the curve where her neck met her shoulder. It was quick and shocking, and her orgasm pulsed harder when she realized what he'd done.

Claiming mark. Holy. Shit. Torren had just claimed her. He'd marked her so the whole world knew she belonged to HavoK. That she belonged to the new Kong. He'd just picked a mate, and this scar was a subtle fuck-you to any gorilla who tried to make him the head of a family group.

He'd picked her instead.

She wanted to cry out his name, just cry and scream in relief, hug him for years, and then have sex again right away, and…and…and…

Torren cupped her head again and lifted her quick, pressed her face against his throat, begging in silence while his dick still pulsed inside of her, filling her with warmth.

She made the mark quick. He'd bled enough today and she didn't want to shred him, but her tiger wouldn't let it be a light mark either. She tore his skin right at a blank space in his tattoos so everyone could see it. She made it deep and rough so it would hopefully heal red and angry-looking, so the people who kept coming after him for the throne could see he didn't belong to the gorillas. He belonged to a rogue tiger who would always have his back, stalking anyone who messed with him. Her claws were his, just like his fists belonged to her. Her teeth were his too, and right now they were the weapon that would tell the world he wasn't up for grabs.

She released his skin and licked the blood off him because the tiger inside of her required that. She needed to clean him, so she did. Over and over until their orgasms had faded to nothing. Until he relaxed into her animalistic affection. Until he was petting his fingertips down her ribs in comforting strokes. Until his skin fused together and stopped bleeding completely.

And then he finished his part of the promise. Easing back, he cupped her cheek and searched her eyes as he murmured, "I'm not running. I'm here."

He kissed her forehead, the tip of her nose…her lips. "I'm right here."

TEN

"This is the most sparkly thing I've ever seen in my life," Torren said, handing her the black sequined duffle bag he'd retrieved from his car.

She always carried extra clothes in her Jem's bag. "Stop looking at it like it's a bug. The bag is so cool. You're about to have your mind blown. Look." When she wiped her hand the opposite way of the sequins, the black sparkles turned pink, her favorite color combination.

"Whoa!" Torren ran his oversize hand down the side of her bag and marveled at the color-change. "It's like a chameleon bag."

"I have shorts that do the same thing. They're

purple and black."

"Mmmmm," he rumbled with a wicked smile. "I'm gonna make you put those on and I'm gonna play with your butt. And your puss—"

"Ew! Don't say that word."

"That's what it is! What do you want me to call it?"

"Lady bits."

"Veto."

"Vagimjam."

"Also veto." Torren was trying to look severe but a smile was tugging at the corners of his mouth.

"Tuna wallet."

He snorted but his eyes were dancing. "Stop."

She was giggling now though, and didn't want to stop. "Sausage—"

"No."

"Sausage cave." Cracking up, arms thrown around her middle, she said, "Pink pouch."

"You're fired. You're not my manager anymore," he said, walking away.

"Wait! I don't have shoes," she rushed out,

struggling into a pair of jeans and a skintight white sweater. It was cold, and snow was raining down from the holes in the roof of the sawmill. "Carry me," she said, arching her eyebrows.

"Woman, you ain't helpless, but I'm gonna do this because I want an excuse to smoosh your sexy body against mine again." He jogged back and gave her his back, bent slightly, and allowed her to climb on him like a koala. "Here, let me have the bag," he murmured, taking it from her. "God, your toes are so little and cute. Next time paint your nails blue."

"Favorite color?"

"Yep."

"I don't have money for a pedicure."

"Chhh, I'll paint them then."

She tensed on his back in excitement. "You will?" she asked loud right next to his ear. He hunched and rumbled a growl. In a whisper scream she repeated, "You will?"

"Yeah, why not?"

"I don't know. You're this big, badass, tatted-up king silverback brawler."

"I also grew up with a sister who liked girly shit. She had trouble making friends because of the hearing impairment, so I was her best friend. I did whatever she wanted. Whatever made her happy. I've had practice painting nails."

"I think that's the sweetest and sexiest story I've ever heard."

"Really?" he asked, stepping carefully through the rubble.

"Yeah. Why did Vyr write HavoK on the sign? That could get you in trouble if the cops come out here. Everyone knows you're HavoK."

"Uhhhh, because this sawmill is mine. Technically."

"What?" she asked, too loud again.

"Vyr bought this place years ago. He was losing control more and more, and he hoped if he picked some mountains, his dragon would see it as his treasure and settle down. When he bought this place, part of his decision to claim territory here was the sawmill right on the edge of the property. I grew up in lumber country."

"You were a lumberjack?"

Torren chuckled. "Yep. In the cold months when I was a teenager, I was up there with the crews, learning my way around the occupation. The manual labor was good for my animal. It kept me tired. But when the fire season came, logging shut down. It's too dangerous to have the machines up there when it's that dry and hot. One spark from the equipment could devastate the area with fire. My dad owned a sawmill in Saratoga, and that's where I worked when I wasn't logging. Vyr wanted to give me a future. He didn't realize the toll on my silverback for being the new Kong , and he thought I would have more time, so he bought this place for me to fix up and start my own business. Do what I know. What makes me happy."

"Logging would make you happy?"

"Stop, Candace. This place isn't my future. My future is ashes and fire. Best you accept that now. I'm devoted to you until the end, but that end will come up fast."

"You stop! Don't talk like that." She scrambled

off his back and winced when she stepped on rubble and lost her balance. Righting herself, she shoved him in the back. The oaf didn't even move. She could've blown a breath on him for all the effect her push had. "You don't claim a girl and say 'Sorry, you've got three and a half days with me, better enjoy it.' Screw that. Try harder. Try for Vyr and for Nox and Nevada. Try for your sister and your parents. Try for the crew. But selfishly, try for me. I don't want you to leave. I'm going to make you stay."

"You can't save me, Candace."

"I didn't offer to save you. You can save yourself, just like I can save myself. But I'm not going anywhere, so if you want to give up and get dragged down to Hell, you'll drag me with you."

"No, I won't."

"You won't have a choice because I'll be tucked against your ribs with my claws dug in. Plus, if you die, it'll hurt me. I don't mean I'll just be sad. We're paired up, and if you go down, I'll go with you now. You're mine," she said, poking a middle finger against his chest. Ouch. "HavoK is mine. Stick around."

"For what?"

"For a family group with me."

Torren's face went completely slack. "W-what?"

"That's what you need, right? A family group?" Candace held her arms out. "Family group of one. Someday you'll make us more."

"What do you mean?"

"Someday you're gonna put a little baby in me. Years from now when we're ready. When you're steady. When you want to see a little baby in my arms, you'll grow our family group. And Vyr and Nox and Nevada will be part of it."

"That's not how family groups work. It's gorillas only."

"I don't care. You're different, Torren. I'm different. Your crew? The Sons of Beasts? They're different. It's not going to look like it would've if you were sitting on the throne of the gorillas. It's going to look better to people like us."

"You…" Torren frowned. "You want a baby with me?"

"Yes. Someday, when you're ready, I want you to put a baby in me. I don't care if she's tiger or gorilla. We're gonna keep you steady. I'm not going to be a dancer forever, Torren. You came in at a bad chapter of my life. You won't be a brawler forever. I came in at a bad chapter for you. Someday, things are gonna be different for you and me, but you have to fight until we get there. And I'll fight with you because someday I do want the life you could give me. I want to see you holding our little baby girl."

"You keep saying baby girl."

"It's just what I imagine when I get lonely. And before you, I was very lonely. I daydreamed about a little baby girl to take care of and give a better life than the one I have. I want to be close to her like my dad was close to me. I couldn't imagine the father though, because I hadn't found you." She jammed her finger at the puncture scars on her neck. "You made bigger promises to me than you realized with this claiming mark."

Torren's wide-eyed gaze dipped to her neck, then to his arm as he held it out. His skin was covered in gooseflesh. It was cold out and he was in a T-shirt, but that man was a furnace. He wasn't cold. He'd just been knocked off balance with her declarations.

She stomped her foot in the snow. "You don't get to quit anymore. Now, you're a mate, and someday you'll be a dad. I'm gonna get you there, but you have to fight with me. No quitting. No quitters in this family group. Too many people need you."

"I—" Torren's voice cracked. He dipped his gaze to the snow and hooked his hands on his hips before he swallowed audibly and tried again. "I would like a baby girl. Someday. A tiger with thin stripes. Orange. Pretty little girl like her momma."

She huffed out a half-laugh, half-sob. He'd just said yes to a family someday. Her face crumpled, and a warm tear trickled down to her jawline. This was something she'd yearned for her whole life. Thickly, she demanded, "Then fight. I like HavoK the way he is. He's a wrecking ball. That's fine. It's up to you to figure out how to let him out and remain sane. For me. For Vyr. For your family back in Damon's Mountains, and Nox and Nevada and that silly, horny swan, and someday, for a little tiger cub with tiny stripes who looks at you like you hung the moon." She shrugged one shoulder up. "Hang the moon, Torren."

"Jesus, woman," he murmured, running his hands through his hair and linking his hands behind his head. "Who's the real wrecking ball? Did you just change the entire path of my life?"

"Get used to it, ya monster. You didn't pick a girl who will sit aside and lose you."

"Clearly. I picked a make-shit-happen girl instead. Gonna make me work."

"I'm high maintenance," she said cheekily.

"Chhh, you don't have to tell me. I know. Got me holding a damn sparkle bag and carrying you over rubble and claiming you and talking future babies."

"I'm not sorry."

"Good. Geez." Torren held his arms out to her. "I'm suddenly hungry enough to eat like six steaks. You stress me out."

She giggled as she melted into the safety of his arms. The man was warm as a campfire, and she snuggled close against his chest. "You eat meat when you're stressed. Perfect man."

Torren snorted. "I like how I can literally have any reaction, and even if it's weird, you just roll with it."

"You aren't weird to me. I understand you. I could go for a steak, too." She rolled her head back and grinned up at him. "Stripping makes me hungry."

Torren belted out laughter and hugged her closer. "Not Changing into a badass tiger and fighting a silverback for your man? That's not what made you hungry? It's the stripping part?"

"Yep!"

Torren shook his head and kissed the top of her hair, lingering there for a few seconds. "I like my life better with you in it. You make my insides feel less dark."

"Good. Feed me."

"High maintenance," he teased her again. But the stunning smile on his face said he liked her just the way she was.

He pulled her by the hand across the parking lot. There was a thin layer of snow, and she looked behind them to see her small footprints next to the giant prints from his boots. She smiled to herself. He was so big next to her, his hand massive around hers, his dominance mountains bigger than hers, and yet she'd never felt safer. His hand was so warm and strong around hers, so steady. She wasn't limping anymore. In fact, she felt completely fine after the fight. Sex with Torren had done wonders for her body. Magical monkey man. And a gentleman monkey because he opened the door to his old, black Camaro and waited for her to buckle up, a slight smile on his face as he watched her, like he thought she was beautiful. And when she clicked her seatbelt into place, he shut the door, made his way around the front of his car, and slid in behind the wheel.

"I like your car." She complimented him as the engine roared to life.

"It was my dad's. He gave it to me for my twenty-first birthday. It's old as dirt, but we kept working on it together, replacing parts, and someday, maybe, I'll give it to our little hellion."

She laughed because, yeah, look at them. A trained dancer turned stripper and a logger turned brawler. Their future kids were definitely going to be hellions.

The drive to Vyr's mansion was short. Torren didn't even ask if she wanted him to take her back to her car, still parked at Jem's. He just drove her to his home. She liked that. He was taking her back to where he was comfortable, inviting her deeper into his life.

And as they crossed the river with the hidden roadway, she got excited. She wasn't tired. Quite the opposite, she was energized from the night with Torren. And she knew it was silly, but she wanted to show Nevada, Nox, and even Vyr the claiming mark Torren had given her. She was proud, and who else would understand its meaning? Only the crew.

But when they pulled into the clearing, blazing red and blue police lights were illuminating the night.

"What the hell?" Torren growled, the steering wheel creaking under his grip.

"Torren, look," she murmured in shock, pointing to the huge hole in the side of the mansion that was billowing smoke.

"Fuck. Vyr must've done it."

She squinted at the officers standing near the two police cruisers. "Thank God. I know one of them. That's Sheriff Thompson. He's good. He helps at the club every time the guys get out of control, and he knows about the fox shifters. He pretends he doesn't, but he does. He has protected the shifters from being outed in Foxburg. He's pro-shifter and understanding. Look, he's just talking to Vyr and Nox, not putting them in handcuffs."

"What about that one?" Torren asked, jerking

his chin at the tall truck of a man standing somberly beside Sheriff Thompson.

"I don't know him. Maybe he's new. Foxburg is a really small town, and the police force has only been three strong as long as I can remember."

"I don't have a good feeling about him."

"Why not?"

"Look at his eyes."

The man flashed them a look, and the headlights of Torren's Camaro shone strangely in his eyes. They reflected like an animal's.

"Shit," she whispered. "Shifter. What does that mean?"

"Let's go find out." Torren threw the car into park on the circle drive. "Stay there."

She'd learned from last time he wouldn't make her stay out of this. But he liked to open doors for her. The man didn't have money for fancy gifts, but he took care of her in the ways he could. In the ways that mattered. He made her feel like the queen he said she was.

He pulled open her door and offered his hand

just like last time. Then he pulled her to his side and they walked across the snow-covered yard to face whatever was happening. Together.

Vyr looked pissed, his face strained and his eyes burning silver with elongated pupils. He was looking everywhere but at Candace, but she didn't understand. Was his anger for her?

"What's going on?" Torren asked in that growly voice that said HavoK was drawn up and ready to beat his chest and charge.

"Once upon a time," Nox started, crossing his arms over his bare chest as he glared at the shifter cop, "a meteor blasted through the wall of Horace's room and woke the whole house with the billowing smoke. And these fart nuggets came to investigate. On private land. When we didn't call them for help."

"First off," the shifter cop growled. "I can hear all your lies. We know that's Vyr Daye, and there was no meteor. The Red Dragon blasted a fireball through the wall of his own bedroom."

"Hi, Sheriff Thompson," Candace said sweetly.

"Everything is fine, really. The boys will get a tarp over the hole and we'll get to work on fixing it tomorrow. I'm sorry you had to come out here, but we're all fine, as you can see." Except where the hell was Nevada? Nox didn't look worried so she forced herself not to worry either.

"Cinnamon—"

"Candace, please. I'm off work and ready to go to bed. It's been a long night."

Sheriff Thompson smiled understandingly. "I'm Officer Thompson now, and this is the new Sheriff of Foxburg, Sheriff—"

"Sheriff Hank Butts," Nox interrupted. "I've nicknamed him Hanky Panky. You're all welcome."

Officer Thompson sighed and closed his eyes. He looked exhausted. "This is Hank Butte. He is the new Sheriff of Foxburg."

"Wait, you were demoted?" Candace asked. She made an apologetic gesture to the giant shifter, who reeked of dominance and fur. Grizzly maybe? Big cat? "I mean, I'm sure you are good at this job, but Sheriff Thompson has been in charge of this town for a long time, and he's very good."

"Not good enough," the shifter said rudely.

"Here's what I think," Vyr said in a voice as cold and smooth as whiskey on the rocks.

"Horace," Torren warned, not giving up his real name.

"I think you're here for me," Vyr said, ignoring Torren. "I think they brought in a specialist when people figured out I was here. Am I right? Something's building? I can feel it. My crew can feel it. I burned some of the woods and people saw the dragon, but it's been quiet since then. Silent. Doesn't make sense. But you," Vyr growled, angling his head. "You make more sense. Polar bear. You've had quite the career."

"Careful, dragon."

"Kicked off force after force…for excessive force. And then you disappeared for the last five years. Where'd you go, Hank Butte? Did you go get yourself some special training somewhere? Training that made you the man for this job?"

Sheriff Butte gave him a toothy, feral smile.

"I'll see you soon, Vyr. Enjoy your night." He nodded once and then sauntered off to his cruiser. The way he'd said that, he might as well have been saying "Enjoy your freedom while you can."

Candace felt sick as she watched the police cruisers pull out of the clearing and disappear into Vyr's woods.

When Candace couldn't even hear the rumble of the car engines anymore, Vyr rounded on her. "You called to me. I was asleep and I had a dream, and in that dream, it was just a voice. Your voice. Calling me to you. You said Torren needed me. I woke up choking on fire."

"Oh, shit," Torren growled, pulling Candace behind him. "Vyr, this is on me. She was scared and saw me getting hurt."

"It was all I could do not to Change and burn this damn town to the ground looking for you."

Nox lifted his hand like he was in grade school. "Actually, I can take some of the credit for stopping the Change."

"You tried to piss on me!" Vyr roared. "You

missed, and now I have to change my bed sheets because they have *urine* on them. I'm so fucking sick of people pissing on me!"

"Well, it worked when Nevada did it! I didn't know what else to do. And P. S.," Nox yelled, "You could say 'Thank you, Nox, for stopping my Change because Torren wasn't here.' I went charging into your bedroom worried because there was a damn fire. You were terrifying and I still tried to stop you! I am the fucking MVP of tonight." Nox bent, picked up a handful of snow, and chucked it at Vyr's face. "You suck and you make a terrible dragon and I'm glad I pissed in your bed." As he walked away, he muttered. "And P. P. S. I'm gonna pee on your fuckin' sheets every time you piss me off, you scaly-lizard-dick-turd-flake." He tossed a middle finger over his shoulder and disappeared into the smoking hole in the wall instead of using the front door.

Vyr stood frozen, his cherry-red face speckled with snow and his silver dragon eyes wide.

Torren cleared his throat. "I think I should take

this opportunity to tell you I got in a fight with a couple of silverbacks tonight. It went bad and one of them drove a Ford Mustang through the front wall of the sawmill. And I bit Candace, and she bit me back, soooo…I think we'll go inside now and let you process this. You know…having a new crew member."

Torren made his way to the hole in the wall while Candace stood there with her face all scrunched up, wishing she had a way with words that would make Vyr look less enraged. "Can I get you a beer? Or…something? Alpha?"

A dinosaur rumble emanated from him as he glared at her. Vyr was terrifying.

"Right. I'll just be inside if you need anything. Sorry about calling you in my head, and the…" She waved her hand at the charred hole in his bedroom wall. A flame blazed up and then died in a bout of bad timing. "Goodnight, Vyr."

And then she followed the boys through the hole and ignored the scent of smoke and Nox's piss that filled Vyr's room.

It hit her as Torren and Nox came back into the room dragging a massive, blue tarp and a long length of rope—she was a part of this. She was welcomed. Invited in. A member. One of them.

The boys worked in silence to get the hole covered, and Nevada came to stand beside her. "I didn't want to talk to the police," she said softly. "I don't like talking to anyone but the boys. And you. You're okay, too."

With a sigh, Candace draped her arm around Nevada's shoulder and they watched the boys.

Nox moved the tarp and shouted outside, "Hey Vyr, can you check on Mr. Diddles?"

Nox and Torren jerked out of the way of a golf ball-sized sphere of fire that blasted through the tarp.

"His name isn't fucking Mr. Diddles!" Vyr yelled.

"I never called him Fucking Mr. Diddles. That's a terrible name!" Nox hollered back.

Vyr let off a long, prehistoric bellow that shook the whole house. Torren sighed tiredly and stared at her like are-you-sure-you're-up-for-this-mess?

But even with the rough ending to the night, she was still here, arm around Nevada, her new friend, with the boys. Claiming mark still tender on her neck, and newly paired with a man she was falling hard for. She wasn't eating a microwave dinner over the sink in her apartment alone, dreading the roach season.

Now, for better or worse, she was part of a crew.

Sure, it was arguably the worst crew in the whole world…but it was hers.

And that counted for a hell of a lot.

ELEVEN

Dad's tiger was the most familiar thing in the whole world. He was a big, powerful, dominant, rogue. He walked gracefully in front of her, the forest alive with cottonwood fluff and flying bugs. Everything was so bright and saturated with the midday light. She didn't recognize these woods, but she didn't mind. Dad was here. Candace was safe.

Her little paw sank in the soft earth into one of Dad's prints. Someday she was going to grow big and strong like him. He paused and looked at her over his shoulder.

I'm here, Dad, sticking close like you taught me.

He was panting, but not from exhaustion. It was hot here. And foggy... No. Smoky. Dad's gold eyes were relaxed, though. Come on, Little Cubby.

Coming, Dad. *Candace bounced forward, determined to be big and tough like him. She rubbed her little body against his leg.* I love you, Dad. I'll always love you. You're the best dad.
Puuuuuurrrrrrr.

He licked roughly up her neck the wrong way, and she shook her head to get rid of the tingly sensation of her fur standing against the grain.

Now it smelled like smoke, and she scowled and sneezed. Gross smell. Not like a regular fire, but something more sinister. Her heart started beating faster, and she was getting a little scared. But Dad still looked steady and wasn't rushing his pace when he began walking again. She felt watched, and when she scanned the smoky woods, there were people standing around, watching them. Men and women, all their eyes glowing—shifters. Dad?

Everything is fine, *his quick glance said.* They're friends.

We don't have friends.

Dad was walking faster now. Gotta keep up. Move little legs!

"You're supposed to be here," a man said.

Candace skittered to a stop and crouched down to her belly. The ferns tickled her tummy. She flattened her ears and hissed because the man was scary. Tall. Muscular. His eyes were glowing green, and on his arm was a giant raven. He walked toward her with a deep limp, then stopped and adjusted his stance. He said it again. "You're supposed to be here. For him."

She didn't understand, but the man and the raven looked off to the left, and when she followed their gaze, her heart stuttered.

There was a massive silverback standing on all fours, tall and proud next to a giant, blue dragon. Kong, Torren's father, and Damon Daye, Vyr's father. And both were watching a small red dragon, standing on the ground, wings tucked, blasting a stream of fire at a half-grown gorilla. Torren. Vyr. Torren shrank back and roared in pain.

Stop, Vyr! You're hurting him!

Vyr clamped his mouth closed, tensed to jump, and beat his wings hard until he was airborne. But then Torren was charging. Fearless Torren. Kong. HavoK. He leapt high in the air and wrapped his arms around Vyr just as he retracted his wings to beat them against the air currents again. His arm was blistered and mangled from the fire but Torren held on tight as they pummeled to the earth. They crashed hard, splitting the ground under their force. The crack in the earth snaked straight to Candace and stopped right at her tiny paws.

"Stop, or you'll hurt me! You'll hurt me, and I'll never be your friend again. I won't be your friend, Vyr. I won't!" Torren bellowed.

Everything froze, the entire scene before her. Torren was still as ice, arms wrapped around the frozen Red Dragon. The man with the raven didn't move a muscle. There was no rustle of leaves, no movement of small forest animals. There was silence. There was stillness.

Dad?

But when she looked for him, he wasn't there anymore. In his place was a white tiger with small stripes and one blue eye, one green.

"Mom?" Candace looked down at herself. Her tiny paws had disappeared. In their place were human hands covered in her black winter mittens. She wore black pants and a black sweater. She was grown. "Mom?" she asked louder.

"I'm sorry I left."

"Why?" she asked, tears burning her eyes. "Why did you do that?"

The smoke was growing thicker, wafting through the woods and covering everything.

The white tiger sat there staring at her with the saddest eyes. Candace could hear her mom's voice so clearly in her head. "I just couldn't stay. You'll do better. You won't be like me. Everything is going to be okay, Little Cubby. But first you have to do something brave."

"What?"

"Help. Your. Man."

And then dragon's fire blasted through the

smoke and swallowed up the white tiger.

"No!" Candace screamed, lurching up in bed.

Bedroom? Yes, she was in a bedroom. She couldn't breathe. She was in bed, not the woods. A mattress on the ground. An old black and white picture of Torren and his family on the wall. A lamp glowing with soft light in the corner by the neatly folded piles of clothes.

She searched the bed, but she was alone. Torren's side was cold. They couldn't have been asleep long because it was still dark out.

A low, vibrating rumble filled the room, and Candace froze in terror. Slowly, she forced her gaze to the red-haired behemoth leaning against the open doorframe. He wore blue linen pajama pants but no shirt. His torso was covered with tattoos, and his arms were crossed over his chest, making his biceps look intimidatingly big. Vyr stared at her with those silver snake eyes. "I saw that dream. Your demons are loud tonight," he murmured in a cold voice.

"D-did I wake you?"

"No. Torren's demon was louder."

"HavoK?"

Vyr nodded once. He angled his face and studied her. "I know he fights. I know he can't help it. I know he's getting sicker. I know I can't stop HavoK from taking his sanity. He gets worse year after year, month after month, and lately, day after day. Why are you here?"

"Because Torren is the keeper of you. And I want to be the keeper of Torren. I want him to stay."

Vyr frowned. "Stay in the Sons of Beasts Crew?"

"No," she whispered. "Stay on this Earth. With me. I want to keep him."

Vyr lifted his chin and stared down his nose at her. "I can see how much you mean your words." He tapped his temple twice. "Usually I hate this power. Hate. It. But just now you became important to me. Stop HavoK from what he's doing to my woods. Bring him home and make him sleep easy. He doesn't do that anymore. Prove you can tame

HavoK, and I'll welcome you into my crew."

"You love him," she rushed out before he could leave. "As a friend. You act cold to everyone, but Torren was always yours to keep safe, wasn't he?"

"Hmm," he rumbled, tightening his arms over his chest. "There are very few dragons left, and none like me. It doesn't matter what HavoK looks like. To me, Torren is my brother. He's a dragon in a gorilla's body." Vyr's eyes blazed a lighter silver as he locked his gaze with hers. "I won't be around forever."

"Don't say that."

"I won't, Candace. I don't talk about this with the crew, but with you, you should know what your role will be when I'm gone."

"What role?"

"Save. Torren. Because when I go, HavoK will turn into the devil himself."

Chills rippled up her legs. She opened her mouth to say more, but Vyr turned abruptly and disappeared into the dark hallway.

Crap. Vyr was alpha here. A reluctant one, but

alpha nonetheless, and if he was leaving, this crew was going to be thrown into turmoil. It would topple the hierarchy and shred the crew, the dominant males especially, from inside their minds outward. Broken bonds were bad for beasts like Torren, Nox, and Vyr.

With a huffed breath, she rushed to grab her jacket and slipped her feet into her snow boots. She was only wearing one of Torren's XL shirts to sleep in, but she didn't want to bother with shoving herself into jeans right now. Not when Vyr had told her HavoK was doing something bad in the woods.

Torren, Torren, Torren, please be all right.

That dream with her dad and mom had messed with her head, and all she wanted was to cuddle up against Torren's chest and feel okay again.

Her unlaced boots made a crunching sound each step she took through the snow. The temperature was dropping. Thanks to the tiger in her middle, the cold only bothered her a little bit. She wrapped her arms around her stomach to conserve warmth as she followed the gorilla prints into the woods. The first streaks of gray illuminated the cloudy horizon, and snowflakes were falling slowly in big clusters. It reminded her of ashes raining down after the eruption of a volcano.

She heard HavoK long before she saw him. Or rather heard his destruction. In the distance, she could see trees shaking violently as he blasted his fists against them, and she heard the beating of his fists against his chest. Carefully, she stepped over logs and brush until she came to the edge of a small clearing. HavoK was destroying a tree. And when he got tired, he sauntered away and beat his chest, little specks of red flinging onto the white snow before he charged the tree again.

"Stop," she murmured.

He didn't react.

"I said stop!" she demanded, approaching slowly.

HavoK roared and pushed off the tree, paced away, chest puffed out, eyes on her, posturing. His eyes were greener than moss after a spring rain, and with every step, his knuckles bled onto the snow.

Before, she could only imagine what these Changes were like for him, but now she saw. She saw the damage. Saw the anger. Saw an animal with too much control.

"Torren," she murmured.

HavoK peeled his glossy black lips over his long canines. "He's not home," HavoK said in that growly voice.

"Why not?"

HavoK spun and picked up a fallen log, then chucked it against another tree with a deafening crack. "Because dreams."

"Bad ones?"

"Always bad." HavoK slapped the side of his head three times and went back to pacing.

She made her way closer. "I had a bad one, too. What was yours about?"

"You. You. You. Tiger getting thrown through the wall. Tiger under that silverback and his fist, and what if I hadn't been fast enough to stop him? I dreamed I wasn't. When I woke up, you were sleeping and I was… I checked if you were breathing. Your Torren wasn't there. Just me."

"My Torren," she repeated softly, closing the gap between them. "And you're my HavoK."

His lip snarled up but fell instantly. His eyes softened, and he stopped the pacing when she reached out for his arm. He allowed her to pull his massive hand from the ground. She searched his eyes for a few moments more before she examined the mess he'd made of his knuckles. "Why?"

"Because I must."

"Why?"

"Because my body needs to stay strong. Because it needs to stay used to pain."

"Why?"

The massive silverback huffed a frozen breath and sat in the snow, straightened his spine, but didn't pull his hand out of hers. "So I can keep you and Vyr and Nox and Nevada safe."

"Not like this. This doesn't just hurt you, HavoK. It hurts Torren. You rip away from him, shove him aside, and the more you do that, the shorter your life will be."

"Don't care. Easier this way."

"For who?"

"Me."

"And what about me? What about your mate? What about your family group? What about your crew?"

HavoK gave his attention to the woods and looked bored. "Only care about you."

"And Vyr."

HavoK slid her a narrow-eyed glance but didn't argue.

"And also Nox and Nevada," she said, because she knew it to be true.

"They're strange. I don't understand them."

Candace giggled. "I don't think anyone understands them, and I think they like it that way." Suddenly, before she could change her mind, she told him, "You're Changing too much. Hey," she murmured, lowering her voice. "Look at me."

HavoK grimaced, but allowed her to cup his face.

"It's too much, and you're hurting Torren. And

the more you hurt him, the more you hurt me."

His breath steamed from him like engine smoke. He looked enormous, strong, and capable. His coal black fur and the dark gray saddle of color on his back contrasted against the white snow. He was a striking creature. He was deadly power meets beauty.

"Family group," HavoK said low.

Candace smiled. "That's me. But you have to work to keep everything together. What would our family group do without you? Who would keep me safe? Who would keep Vyr safe from the world, and the world safe from Vyr?"

"Who would beat the shit out of Nox?"

Candace snorted. "That, too. We need you. I need you, but you have to do better than this. You don't keep yourself in check, and you push for more and more power, and what does that do for you?"

"Feels good."

"Up until the point you lose everything."

HavoK scratched his lip and let off a low, unhappy-sounding rumble. "I don't like rules. I like to make them or break them."

"Then we'll call it compromise. Three."

"Three times a day?" HavoK barked.

"That's way more than any other shifter I've ever met, so quit your belly-achin'."

"That's half the time I get now."

"But consider the quality of time, HavoK. You've spent how long out here beating up trees? Is this the time you fight for? Time away from me?"

"Four."

"Three," she said in a stern voice.

HavoK opened his mouth and roared, then paced away and back. "You want Torren."

"I want both sides of Torren. The man and you."

"No, because you try and tuck me away. I checked if you were breathing this morning. Me. Last night, I pulled that silverback off you. Me!"

"I love you!"

HavoK skidded to a stop in the snow, smearing red with his knuckles. After a few loaded seconds, he demanded, "Explain love."

The wind was picking up and it was getting

colder, so she pulled her jacket tighter around her torso. "Okay…love is worrying over someone. It's putting them above yourself. It's smiling when they smile because their happiness makes you happy. It's wanting a future with them and working to make them okay so you can both have that future. It's wanting to know if they are sad so you can hug them and make it better. It's crying when they say something nice because you feel joy they really see you when no one else does. It's not being invisible. It's sleeping beside them and having a bad dream, so you wake up to check if they're breathing. Because if they weren't, it would feel like you weren't breathing. It's a feeling that when everything is falling apart, they can fix it just by looking at you. A single look, and you know everything will be okay. Love is feeling safe with someone."

While she'd spoken, HavoK had stopped fidgeting and had become still like a statue. His attention had drifted to her mouth and stayed there as she formed her words. And when she was finished, he frowned. "You feel these things about me?"

With a smile, Candace nodded. "And it's also standing out in the freezing cold at dawn just on the off-chance I can bring you back to warm me up in bed."

His frown grew deeper. "You shiver."

In an effort to keep him on track, she made her voice stern again and said, "Three times a day. No more. I need both sides of you to be steady because I've lost a lot. I lost my mom and my dad, and now it's just me out in the world if you aren't here to tether me to you, and to the crew. I don't want to be alone again. Don't let that happen."

She turned on her heel and made her way back through the woods, following the tracks she'd made. Already they were filling with snow. It hurt walking away, but she'd put everything out there, and now the animal half of the man she loved would need to make his own decisions.

Quit or stay, just like the decision she'd had to make.

"Candace," Torren said.

Startled by his human voice, she jerked her gaze up from the snow where she'd been carefully stepping. And there he was. Skin pale, tattoo ink stark against the snowy background. His knuckles were already healing but still looked painful. His eyes were hollow and exhausted.

"You've been fighting with yourself," she said.

He nodded once, slowly. "Different kind of fight from last night. The physical ones are easier."

"Are you there at all? When HavoK takes over. Do you see and feel what's happening?"

"Sometimes more than others. Sometimes not at all. Sometimes it's like I went to sleep and I wake up and my body hurts." His bare feet made deep prints in the snow as he approached.

He slid his arms around her and hugged her tight, lifting her off her feet. "You're terrifying."

"Me? Why?" she asked, wrapping her arms and legs around him, and holding on. She didn't want him to put her down. Hell, she could stay like this forever. Just them and the silent falling snow and the winter woods of Vyr's Mountains.

"Because now I have something to lose. Something big. Before, I had already accepted the break HavoK was making in me. Now I want to fight it, but I don't know how. You're scary because I can let you down, and I don't want to. I had accepted my fate, but now I don't want what's happening to me, or to my gorilla."

"Then stay," she said simply. Candace eased back and ran her fingertips down his beard. "Stay with me. You and HavoK both. We're going to figure it out, me and you. And the crew."

Torren snorted. "That entire crew is fucked up and not at a point where they can help anyone else."

"Not anyone else, just crew." She grinned and slid down his body, settled on her knees in the snow but kept her eyes on him.

There was a wicked twinkle in Torren's green eyes now. "What are you doing?"

"Tempting you to try harder."

"Mmmm. I like when you say harder." He snarled up his lip and gripped the back of her hair roughly.

Sexy, dominant man. He had so many layers. Rugged brawler on the outside and vulnerable man desperate to stay steady on the inside. Big, muscular, tattooed beast, body humming with power as his eyes sparked an even brighter green. He was hard already, so she gripped him and slid her hand down his shaft. Torren let off a soft rumbling sound and urged her face closer.

She'd already won. He didn't look tired and beaten anymore. He even *felt* stronger to her again. Confident. Stable. Hungry.

Candace slid her mouth over him, hand at his hilt because he was too big to take all at once.

He gave off a shaky, "Fuuuck," as she applied more pressure with her tongue.

She kept the pace steady, and he was good. He was gripping her hair but not forcing her. He was letting her do what she wanted. Good mate. She wanted to take care of him right now and make him forget about losing control.

When Candace dug her nails into his powerful

outer thigh, he grunted a sexy noise, and his muscles twitched. Her name came like a prayer to his lips as she pushed him closer to release. He was moving with her now, body shaking, muscles flexed, dick hard in her mouth. He tasted so good, and she looked up at him just to see the expression of pure intensity as he watched her suck him off. She felt powerful, having such control over a monster of a man like this. He might be the new king, the new Kong, but she was his queen, and queens had more power than people realized. It was subtle power. Quiet power.

Torren's hand gripped her hair harder, and she moaned at how good it felt. His little signs of lost control set her body on fire. God, she loved turning him on. He thrust deeper into her throat. Deep, deep, deep and then he pulled out of her mouth suddenly with a muttered curse. He dropped to his knees and pushed her back against the snow, shoved her sleep shirt up her thighs, grabbed his dick, and pushed inside of her. He didn't prepare her for his size, but she was ready. She'd been so excited while she'd had her mouth on him, her body had been begging for him to bury himself just like this. He filled her, stretching her in an instant as he drove deep, then deep again and again.

The pressure was building so fast it was blinding. All consuming. She raked her fingernails down his back and wasn't careful. She dug deep, and they both arched their backs. When Torren looked back down at her, his eyes were on fire. Hungry, hungry man, and she was the one who fed his soul. She could see it. See her value as he laid his weight on her and pounded into her, faster, harder. His hand drifted from her hip to her thigh, and he yanked her leg up higher, then gripped it hard enough that his fingers dug in. It felt so good. Pleasure and pain. Rough boy. Fuck, how had she lived without this connection for so long? Without Torren?

He slammed into her harder, and she was done. She was a grenade, and he'd pulled the pin on her the second he'd slid into her. Her body shattered around him, pulsing deep and hard just as he bucked into her and froze. His dick throbbed deep inside her, filling her with warmth. He pushed in again—throb—again—throb. She threw her head back and moaned as her orgasm intensified.

Suddenly, before he was done with his release, Torren yanked out of her and took himself in hand, shoved her shirt up her stomach, and finished across her bare chest.

"You're *mine*," he growled, his face twisted and feral. "My mate. My family group."

Sexy. The perfect balance of monster and man, and yeah, she *was* his. She had been since the second she saw him in Vyr's mansion.

Her animal had picked, and she'd always been a loyal soul. No matter what the future held, their fates were tied in an impossible knot now. And she had no regrets, because this ache in her chest was something she thought she would never feel. It was something she thought would never happen to a damaged girl like her.

He was building their bond, one touch at a time. One sigh, one smile, one laugh, one nickname, one good experience, one hard experience at a time. He'd let her see the gritty parts, and deep down, she knew he didn't do that for anyone else.

He was king on his own terms.

And from here on, she would be his queen on hers.

TWELVE

"I have a surprise for you," Candace said, smiling at Torren's profile as he drove them through Vyr's woods.

Torren jerked his gaze to hers, but she couldn't read his expression. "Are you pregnant?"

"What?" she asked too loud. "No!"

There was a flash of something—disappointment—right before he forced a smile and said, "I was just kidding." That sounded like a lie, though.

After a few stunned moments, she murmured, "Torren, is that something you want?"

He shrugged and turned up the rock music in his

Camaro. "It's whatever."

Candace adjusted the box in her lap and turned in the seat to see him better. He'd carefully constructed his face into a mask of ambivalence. She turned the volume down. "Don't throw this conversation away. I'm not opposed to having a baby. I just didn't know you would want to try so soon. You surprised me."

Torren's Adam's apple dipped into his thick throat as he draped one hand over the steering wheel and slid the other to her thigh, his favorite way to drive. "It's something I think about. I know we're new to being mates and you're just moving in. We're figuring out our lives together and with the crew. But sometimes when HavoK feels out of control, like he's going to break your three-Changes-a-day rule, I think of you holding a little baby. A baby I put in you. And the gorilla settles because he wants that someday, too."

Candace was completely stunned. And elated. She wanted to cry from happiness. It had been three weeks since he'd claimed her, and today had been one of the happiest days of her life already because he'd asked her to let go of the lease on her little, bug-infested apartment and make a home with him in the mansion. She'd practically been living there anyway since that first fight with those silverbacks. Since then, he'd secured a job running security at Jem's, made her job and life safe without chasing off customers, and she'd been at every fight, at his back, supporting him as he did what he had to do to keep HavoK steady. Days were spent with the man she'd fallen in love with, and with the crew. Day by day, she was growing closer to these crazies that she somehow understood. Her life was moving in the right direction, finally, because of Torren. And now he'd just told her he wanted to put a baby inside her. She'd asked her questions and done her research. Torren was a big, dominant gorilla shifter, and him saying he was ready to add to their little family group was a big deal. He really was trying to stay strong for her.

She slipped her hand over his and admitted something she'd felt for a while. "I know we haven't said it out loud yet, but I love you, you know?"

Torren eased onto the brakes and pulled them to a slow stop, careful of the icy road. His smile was stunning as he looked over at her. "You told me the other day."

Candace gasped. "When?"

"In your sleep."

"Don't play."

"I'm serious. You talk in your sleep, and it's so fucking cute. You know how I know you love me?"

"How?"

"Because even in your sleep, when you don't have to touch me, you do. And you tell me sweet things. And you purr."

Candace's cheeks heated with mortification. "I do not."

"You so do. I fucking love it. Sometimes I wake up just to ask you questions or watch you sleep. Listen to you purr when I touch your hip or brush your hair out of your face. I told you I love you, too. You did this little smile and whispered, "I know.""

He made a ticking sound behind his teeth. "Wildcat, you think you know everything—even when you're unconscious."

"Well, I do," she said, ducking his tickling fingers as she laughed. She settled against the back of the seat and muttered, "Crap. Saying that for the first time is a big deal and I slept through it." She frowned at the front window. "You distracted me. I had a surprise and you derailed it."

A deep chuckle rumbled in Torren's chest. "Okay, I'll be good. Give me."

Candace pulled the three twenties out of her back pocket and handed it to him.

Torren frowned at the money and shook his head. "I don't understand. I'm not asking you to pay rent. I've got us."

"It's for Genevieve."

His bright gaze jerked to her face. He searched her eyes for a few moments before he took the twenties slowly. "Are you serious?"

"Yeah, I've been doing good at work, and I paid the bills for this month. Now that I'm not paying for the apartment, I can help with your sister's cochlear implant fund. I mean, I know it's not a lot—"

"Stop. This is a lot, Candace." He shook his head and looked at her like she was everything. That expression on his face? It made butterflies flap around in her stomach. "I know how hard you work for every penny, and I know what it costs you to work that job. This?" He lifted the sixty bucks. "This means more than I can even tell you."

"We'll do it as a team," she said softly. "Someday she's gonna hear your voice, and I'll be so proud of you for getting there."

"We'll do everything as a team. I can't wait for you to meet my sister and her mate, Greyson. And my parents. They all love you already because I can't stop talking about you. You've changed my whole life for the better."

"Even though I get stripper glitter all over everything?"

Torren belted a laugh. "My life is a lot more sparkly, that's for sure."

He leaned over the seat and cupped her neck,

pulled her to him, and pressed his lips against hers. Usually they were fire and gasoline when they touched, but sometimes, on occasion, Torren would go all soft like this. For her. She loved him both ways. She loved him just as he was.

There was something so freeing about loving someone just as they were, mess and all, and knowing they would return that acceptance in kind. What a beautiful thing not to have to ever pretend. What was the point when Torren was okay with everything? Her job, her animal, her emotional days, her damage, her fear of losing him. He looked at those things like he thought they were beautiful, and she did the same for him. His fighting, his inner beast, his protectiveness, his devotion to Vyr, his damage. He was perfect to her, shaped exactly right to match her unconventional edges.

He sipped at her lips for a long time, and she melted into him. Let him take his time, let him keep them slow, while she reveled in his soft touches on her cheek, her neck, her hand, her thigh.

But there was this moment when chills rippled

up her arms. And when Torren eased away with a frown, she knew he'd felt it, too.

He scanned the woods out the window and turned the radio all the way down. He sat there frozen, just like her, listening for something just beyond their heightened senses.

"I feel watched," she admitted on a breath.

"Same," Torren rumbled. He rolled down his window and rested his elbow on the open frame, chewed the corner of his thumbnail as he stared out into the woods, listening. "It's too quiet."

"It's always quiet in the winter, though," she said optimistically.

"Mmm," he murmured. He eased onto the gas, but as they drove, he kept his window down and his attention on the woods like she did.

There was nothing out of the ordinary, though. No tracks, no movement, and the closer they got to the mansion, the less her instincts blared.

"Animal maybe?"

"Maybe," Torren said. He flicked two fingers toward the house where Vyr was sitting on the roof, eyes on the woods, one knee bent, one leg dangling over the edge of the gutter. "But then why is the Red Dragon watching the woods, too?"

"Okay. Playing the devil's advocate, Vyr sits up there a lot, and I have a theory about it. I think the ground isn't his home. It's not his happy place. He only allows himself to shift every three weeks, right? Imagine if you forced HavoK to stay silent for three weeks at a time. You would feel all broken up and confused. I think Vyr sits up in the air because it makes his dragon more comfortable. Plus, look. The rest of the crew doesn't seem concerned." She pointed to where Nox and Nevada were sitting in duct-taped lawn chairs in the snow, facing each other, spitting a piece of gum back and forth between them, catching it in their mouths. They cheered each other on each time they caught it.

"God, their love is so weird," Torren muttered.

"Yep." Candace scrunched her face up. "I feel like we could take them, though."

Torren was staring at them with narrowed eyes.

"I was just thinking the same thing. Do you have a piece of gum?"

Candace peeled into giggles. Of course, Torren would be up for playing. He was good at that, and highly competitive with Nox for reasons she would probably never fully understand. "Sorry, fresh out."

She didn't even try to open her own door. A, the moving box in her lap was full of her collection of romance books and was heavy. And B, she'd learned early on that Torren liked to open doors for her. All doors, and he pulled out her chair for her at restaurants, even if it was just a fast food place. And any chance he got, he liked to carry her things. He'd explained he would never be able to buy her a lot of material things, so he liked to take care of her in the ways he could. It was really sweet and made her feel special every time he did, so her smile stretched her face as he jogged around the front of his ride and opened her door. He pulled the box out of her lap as if it weighed nothing and waited for her to grab a stack of clothes from the back of his car. This was the last load from her apartment, so the back was stuffed with mostly odds and ends they'd left until last to transport.

"I made dinner!" Nox called as they made their way to the front door.

"I'm not eating whatever you cooked," Torren muttered. "You burn everything."

"By 'made dinner' I mean I bought pasta from that new Italian place in town. Crew dinner! Page sixty-nine in the Manners and Shit book: spring for food every once in a while."

"Plus, I like when we all eat together," Nevada said. "And I'm tired of instant noodles. The bills are paid this month, so let's celebrate. We even got a box of wine. Thirty-four glasses of crisp white for eleven dollars."

"I like crew dinners, too," Candace admitted. "Feels like those fucked-up, dysfunctional family meals on funny television shows."

"Exactly!" Nevada exclaimed excitedly. "That's what I was telling Nox just yesterday!"

"Uh, yeah, I remember that conversation," Nox muttered, staring at the open *Manners & Shit* book he'd pulled from his pocket.

"Lie," Nevada called him out.

"In my defense, I'm pretty sure that was around the time you said the word 'blow,' and all I could think of was your mouth on my d—"

"Does your mind ever get out of the gutter, Nox?" Vyr asked from the roof.

"The gutter is the best place for the mind to be," Nox explained primly. "It's dark, quiet, and wet—"

"Stop. Talking," Vyr demanded. There was steel and order in his words, and Nox choked on his retort. Tried again but failed to push a word out, so he lifted a middle finger instead.

"Someday I'm gonna bite off both of your favorite fingers," Vyr muttered. "We need to eat fast if we're going to do dinner."

"Why?" Torren asked, turning toward him before he reached the front door.

His gaze was intense on the Red Dragon, who only shrugged up one shoulder and responded, "Storm's coming."

Torren's jaw clenched. "What does that mean?"

Vyr's only answer was to stare with dead eyes at Torren and point to the sky. Indeed, the clouds were dark gray and churning above them. Foxburg was supposed to get four inches of snow tonight.

Torren let off a frustrated snarl and spun on his heel, made his way into the house. But Candace still stood there, looking up at Vyr. He dragged his gaze to her and said, "Remember what I told you, Candace. Remember your role. Don't let the devil out." He held her trapped in that silver dragon gaze for a couple of heartbeats and then gave his attention back to the woods.

"What was that about?" Nevada asked.

Nox was frowning up at Vyr suspiciously.

Under the pile of clothes, Candace's hands shook, but she kept her poker face and shrugged. She couldn't say words or they would be busted as lies, so she scrambled in after Torren and hoped he hadn't heard Vyr's cryptic message to her.

Her role? To stop Torren from going ape-shit when Vyr disappeared. Something was wrong. Something was *really* wrong, and she had a gut-deep instinct that the storm Vyr was talking about had nothing to do with clouds and everything to do with the watched feeling she had felt in the woods.

She and Torren unloaded the car quickly, but in silence. He seemed lost in his own head, probably worried about his friend. Each time they passed through the kitchen to make another run to the car, Nox stopped heating up food to stare at her. The entire crew was feeling this, so when the soft hum of an engine sounded outside, it wasn't surprising at all for her. From the somber looks on the crew's faces, for them either.

"Methinks Damon Fucking Daye has been up to no good," Nox muttered as they all watched the blue and red police lights slowly approaching through the woods.

"Why isn't Vyr running?" Candace asked. Out the window, she could see his leg still dangling from the roof.

"He said this was the last place he would run to," Torren said in a gruff voice. "This is where he wants to stand his ground."

"Are we fighting?" Nevada asked in a meek voice as three more police cruisers and a news van appeared in the clearing.

Torren growled out, "New Sons of Beasts Crew motto: fight everything."

Nox was already peeling off his shirt before the boys got to the front porch. Sheeeyit. Candace bolted after them. The boys would go knuckles first and ask questions later, but she knew most of the police force in this town. Maybe she could talk them down. Plus, this crew couldn't afford a repeat of Covington. That news van meant cameras. Was it even legal to have a news crew present for an arrest? This felt like a violation of privacy.

"Torren!" she called, running to catch up. The boys were speed-walking!

"Nox, wait!" Nevada called from right behind her.

It was Vyr who stopped them, though. He jumped off the roof gracefully with no impact, as if he had flown, but Vyr didn't have his wings right now. That man hid a lot of power, even from his own crew. He blurred to nothing and reappeared right in front of Torren and Nox. "Let them have me. No more fighting, no more running. My father wants this…" Vyr inhaled deeply, and for the first time since she'd known him, Candace witnessed pain in Vyr's eyes. "So okay. Dad wins. The humans win."

"What? No, fuck that!" Torren yelled as a half circle of police cruisers surrounded them. "You're fine."

"I'm dangerous."

"You're in control!"

"As long as I don't shift! It was different when I wasn't alpha, Torren. I was different! Now I have to think about the good of the crew."

Torren shoved him hard in the chest, but Vyr barely moved. "So leaving without a fight is your solution? That's how you take care of your crew?"

"Yes. Because I want you to live. I don't want war. There are consequences to being what I am, and it's time to pay that. And I won't pay with your blood."

"This is fucked up," Nox murmured, arms crossed over his chest.

"On your hands and knees!" Sheriff Butte yelled, a high-powered rifle trained on Vyr. There were a couple dozen other officers in similar stances.

"Our crew will fold without you!" Nox bellowed, his face going red.

"You'll be fine," Vyr argued.

"You're wrong," Torren gritted out. "I won't be fine."

"It's one year—"

"In *shifter prison*, Vyr!" Torren yelled. "You get that, right? You know what that place is like? It's not three square meals a day and working out and catching up on reading. They'll *hurt* you. You won't come back."

"I will."

"You won't and you know it." Torren's entire body was shaking, and his eyes were such a bright green they were hard to look at. He smelled like fur. He reeked of HavoK. "If you're lucky enough to survive it, they're gonna change you, Vyr."

Face blazing red, Sheriff Butte yelled, "I said down on your knees!"

"Torren," Candace warned, sinking slowly to her knees in the snow beside him. "Do what Vyr says. He's alpha."

"He ain't actin' like it," Nox said. "And I don't see him goin' down to his knees either."

Beside him, Nevada was already down in the snow, tugging on her mate's hand, bright gold fox eyes begging him to join her.

Two cameras were trained on them, and a reporter was narrating what was happening. What the hell? Vyr wasn't even fighting.

"Hey! Get those cameras out of here!" Candace yelled. "That's not right. You shouldn't be here. We're cooperating."

"Fuck cooperation," Torren growled.

"On your knees," Vyr demanded. The order in that command rippled through their bonds and stole Candace's breath away. Nox buckled immediately and slammed to his knees so hard the snow beneath him exploded in a plume of white.

Torren grunted in pain but stayed upright on locked legs, right between Vyr and the weapons that were trained on him.

Vyr stepped around him and held his wrists out to Sheriff Butte. "I'm not running, I'm not fighting, let's get this done and leave my crew alone. They've done nothing wrong."

"False statement, Red," Sheriff Butte said, handing his weapon to the lady officer beside him. He approached with a pair of massive handcuffs. "Torren Taylor, you are under arrest for an illegal fighting and gambling ring. We've got video proof. Now your people betrayed you, like you betrayed them."

"What?" Vyr asked.

"We're not here for you, Dragon. We're here for the silverback. Dax Meyers sent us clear video footage of an illegal shifter fight at the old mill. Two boars have come forward and made statements too. He's been setting up fights for months. We've taken pictures of the blood on the floor. Taken evidence. You're fucked, *HavoK*."

"No, no, no," Vyr snarled. "He only fights because he has to. He didn't set up an illegal ring. He has rights."

"He's a shifter," Butte argued.

"So are you, you fuckin' traitor!" Nox yelled.

"Get up," Vyr ordered the crew.

Candace gasped when her body lurched upward. Vyr was backing away, hand across Torren's chest to bring him along. "It's me you want, not Torren."

"Nope, we're really here for the gorilla. Get on your fucking knees, Torren."

"Please, please," Candace begged, pushing on Butte's chest. "He can't go behind bars. He won't do well in there. He needs the crew." Torren would go straight HavoK in a cell. It would be torture.

Butte gave an odd, wild smile in the moment before he wrenched her hands behind her back.

"Ow!" she cried as her shoulder ripped and burned.

"Get your fuckin' hands off her!" Torren bellowed.

And then all hell broke loose. Nox shot up in front of Torren and shoved his chest back hard, but HavoK was already unstoppable. The silverback ripped out of Torren, and it was all Nox could do to get himself and Nevada out of the way as he charged at the sheriff.

The sound of gunfire popped off. Two bullets hit HavoK's massive arm, but he didn't slow at all. More gunfire, but this had a different tone. Candace screamed as a dozen red-feathered darts hit Torren's body. Nox and Nevada were hit too, and in an instant, all three hit the ground.

"Change and I'll kill you," Butte murmured against Candace's ear as he wrenched her arms back at a worse angle.

She hissed at Butte as her eyes watered. "Torren!" she screamed. He roared and arched his back against the ground, face contorted with pain.

His body was breaking slowly, bones snapping, muscles twisting and reshaping.

"Oh, my gosh," she whispered in horror.

"Give them another round, but don't hit Vyr,"

Butte demanded. His voice went strange when he said loudly, "The meds won't suppress his dragon."

"Lie," she called him out.

He ripped her arm upward, and she grunted in pain, but she didn't lose her train of thought. "Vyr, he's lying. They aren't darting you on purpose. What's happening? Vyr!"

The dragon shifter was standing on the edge of the chaos, his eyes drifting from Torren, to Nox, to Nevada, and back to Torren as they writhed in pain. Vyr looked bigger, all puffed up, veins sticking out on his arms and neck. His face was red with fury, and his eyes were silver with elongated pupils. A deep rumble emanated from him and shook the ground beneath her feet.

"Get ready," Butte said quietly into a radio at his shoulder.

Who the fuck was he talking to?

Frantically, Candace looked around. She squinted and searched as far into the woods as she could. There was movement everywhere. Vyr's Mountains were full of people dressed in black with thick vests, helmets, and high-powered rifles. The rumble of heavy equipment drowned out the forest sounds. Tanks? Shit.

"Candace," Torren choked out. He was halfway through the Change the meds were forcing. Whatever they'd shot him with was Turning him human again. He looked like he was in so much pain, teeth clenched, face strained, body contorting, breaking. Breaking like her heart was to watch him in agony. Four officers ripped him off the ground. "Candace," he tried again. "They're going to kill him."

And everything made sense now in this moment of perfect clarity. They didn't care about arresting Torren for fighting. That was the ploy. They were using Torren to poke the dragon. To agitate him into Changing. To turn into the Red Dragon so they could have the excuse to unleash Armageddon on him.

They weren't here to arrest anyone. Vyr wasn't going to shifter prison. They were here to eliminate him.

Torren was in his full human form now, and he pushed upward, eyes on Vyr as he tried to reach him, but there were too many holding him back. More and more officers piled on him as he inched his way toward Vyr. More were throwing themselves on Nox too, and Nevada was pinned down by the lady officer with a handgun trained on the back of her head.

"Vyr!" Torren yelled. "Don't Change! Vyr! Look at me! Don't. Change!"

Inch by inch, Torren was being dragged backward toward a black SUV.

Don't let the devil out. That's what Vyr had told her, but the only devil she saw was in Vyr's eyes as he watched his crew under attack.

Torren was being restrained by eight people but was still making ground toward Vyr, his face desperate as he begged his best friend not to Change. As he tried to save Vyr's life. They probably had a dozen missiles trained on the Sons of Beasts right now, just waiting for the Red Dragon to rise up.

Nox was fighting hard too, struggling against the pile of humans detaining him.

Nevada's face was still shoved in the snow, but she was screaming for Vyr not to Change, over and over. "Don't Change, they'll kill you. Don't Change, Vyr. Do you hear me? They'll kill you!"

Torren would never be okay again if they killed Vyr. He was the keeper of the Red Dragon, and she was the keeper of the new Kong. She had to do something. She had to do *anything*.

Vyr's chest heaved, and he blasted a stream of fire from his human mouth to the nearest police cruiser. It exploded with a deafening sound, but not even that drowned out the awful sound of his enormous, tattered, fire-red wings ripping out of his back. Vyr lifted his clawed hand into the air, and then he flicked his fingers and the second police cruiser slammed into a tree with such force, the impact vibrated through her chest.

What the hell? Vyr could control matter? No, no, no, he shouldn't let the humans see this. Shouldn't let the cameras capture his true power.

"Vyr!" she screamed. "Stop!"

Fucking polar bear that kept her pinned. She had a plan, but it was going to get her hurt and possibly killed. But there was a chance she could stop this if she was fast enough. Vyr was fighting the Change, but the Red Dragon was coming out of him whether he wanted it or not.

"Torren, do you remember the first time Vyr burned you?" she called out. *Please, let him understand.*

"Yes, I remember! Candace!" Torren yelled. There was understanding and desperation in his eyes in the moment they locked onto each other. "Do it."

"Get a dart gun!" she yelled. She didn't know if she was throwing that order out there for Torren, Nox, or Nevada. It didn't matter who got to one, just that one of them did. "Shoot him!" Candace kicked backward as hard as she could, and gasped at the impact her foot made with Butte's shin bone. His grip faltered as he bellowed in pain. She ripped out of his hands and spun, slashing her claws across his face viciously.

She bolted, because Vyr wasn't himself anymore. There was no humanity in his gaze, just the promise of cold-blooded vengeance. Time slowed to a crawl as she sprinted for him. His crimson wings, tattered on the edges, with rips and holes as though he'd been in a hundred battles, stretched across the entire clearing. His body was shaking, blurring, right on the edge of the Change, and she was running out of time. He beat his wings and was airborne in the moments Candace reached him.

She could feel Butte right behind her. Feel his breath on her skin and hear his growl. She wasn't being chased by a man anymore. If she turned around, she would see a monster polar bear hunting her.

Monster behind her, monster in front of her, and she had to choose a death—teeth or fire.

The fire was hers in a way though, right? It belonged to her alpha, to her crew, to her mate. And she would do anything for Torren.

Fire it was.

"Don't let the devil out," she gritted through clenched teeth just to keep her courage.

She leapt through the air just as Vyr's body swelled and his clothes ripped, and blood-red scales covered him. She was good at jumping, thank the tiger. And she was good with her claws as she wrapped her arms around his neck and her legs around his body as best she could.

And she recalled Torren's story, recalled the dream, and she said the words that had stopped his fire all those years ago. "Stop or you'll hurt Torren! You'll hurt him, and he'll never be your friend again. He won't be your friend, Vyr. He won't!"

The wind was deafening as he lifted them higher, and something exploded with great force right above them. A missile? Vyr's dragon rippled out of him, growing impossibly big. Candace screamed and held onto the slick scales of his elongating neck, clawing desperately for purchase.

Higher and higher they rose. In horror, she looked down at the ground just in time to see Nox with a dart gun, unleashing hell in their direction as Torren blasted his fists against the crowd, covering Nox's back and buying him precious seconds. Pain pricked her back in two spots, and as she lost her grip on the dragon, she shrieked. Her breath was stolen as she fell from the sky and back to earth, and she wasn't coming alone. A single red-feathered dart was stuck in Vyr's neck, right where he was missing a scale. Nox had damn good aim. When Vyr roared, he blistered her skin with the heat of his fire as he sprayed it across the woods and fell with her.

Even if she survived the fall, she wouldn't live through Vyr crushing her body under his monstrous weight. And because she knew it was the end, and because she wanted to be brave, she yelled out, "Torren, I'm sorry!" and hoped to God he understood. Sorry she couldn't save his friend, sorry she couldn't save herself, sorry his life would be darker because she hadn't been enough. She was sorry she hadn't saved him because now HavoK would drive them into the ground to cope.

Just before impact, she flinched in on herself and closed her eyes, but she didn't hit like she'd expected to. She was blasted from the side and went sailing through the air so fast her breath was sucked from her lungs. Torren's strong arms were around her. He did his best to shield her from the impact with his body when they hit the earth.

Vyr nearly slammed a wing onto them, but lifted at the last second, and as he shattered inward, jerking and twitching as he shrank, he arched his long neck back and spewed fire into the air with a deafening screech. Smaller and smaller he became until the dragon roar became a man's scream. Vyr fell to his knees in the snow, arms out, body flexed, wings retracting into his body as he stared at the sky with gritted teeth.

"Can you walk?" Torren asked in a rush.

"Y-yes." She hoped she could at least.

"Good girl." Torren righted her quickly and pulled her by the hand.

Too fast because she stumbled. Her body wasn't working right, and she retched. Maybe it was the darts in her back. She couldn't even feel her tiger right now. She felt completely empty. It was terrifying being so alone in this body for the first time in her life.

Torren didn't stop running until they stood in front of Vyr. And then Nox and Nevada were here, blocking their alpha from the weapons that were trained on him, and from whatever hid in the woods that Butte had organized to end the Red Dragon.

The clearing was eerily silent as officers stood in clusters, faces confused, eyes flickering to each other, and then back to the crew, weapons trained on them.

Butte was Changed back and wore a pair of black cargo pants. He looked furious and was saying something low into the radio on his shoulder.

"Vyr Daye, you're under arrest for the destruction you caused in Covington," he called, making his way toward them. "And for the destruction of two police cruisers today."

"Fuck you, Butte," Torren spat.

"Torren," Vyr rumbled. "It's fine. I'm ready.

You'll take Alpha while I'm away." He arched his attention to Candace. "You. Welcome to the Sons of Beasts Crew. You have a job to do, and don't forget it for a second while I'm gone. Keep. Torren. Steady."

Candace blinked back burning tears. It was a confusing moment. She'd just been welcomed to the crew by her alpha, but he was about to leave and cripple them. And she was worried about him. "I don't think you should go alone," she murmured. "They just had a plan in place to kill you, Vyr. You can't trust them to get you to the shifter prison alive."

"No, I can't." Vyr stood slowly and winced like his body hurt. "But I can trust *him* to escort me there safely." He flicked his fingers at an approaching black SUV that was picking its way through the chaos. As it pulled around, the back window rolled down Damon Daye sat somberly in the back.

"Aw fuck," Butte muttered when he looked in that direction. He leaned over to the radio on his shoulder and murmured, "Abort mission and back way off. The Blue Dragon just got here. I repeat, abort all plans."

"Sorry, Sheriff Butts," Nox said, resting his hands on his hips. "If you fuck with Damon's kid, he'll snuff your entire family out of existence. If I was you, and I would hate to be you because your name is Hanky Panky and your polar bear is hideous, I would make sure Vyr gets where he's going in one piece. I mean if you like breathing and all."

Sheriff Butte handcuffed Vyr roughly and shoved him toward one of the remaining cruisers.

"Alpha," Torren called. "What's our play?"

"No play," he called over his shoulder. "You're alpha now. Keep the crew intact. Try not to fuck up too much. Wait for me. One year and I'll be back." He tossed Torren a look over his shoulder that Candace couldn't read, but a thousand things seemed to pass between them in a matter of moments before he was shoved roughly into the back of a police cruiser.

"Candace Sumner," Damon Daye called to her formally. He had silver dragon eyes like Vyr, but dark hair gone gray at the temples. He was striking as a man and emulated pure confidence when he spoke. "You did more than you realize. Your late-father's medical debts will be paid by the end of the day. Torren, I've made a donation to your sister. Her surgery is now covered with the help of all the crews. Use the money you've been saving to make something of yourself. You heard Vyr. You're alpha until he comes home." He gave a slight, sad smile. "Fix up the sawmill. Give your dad some competition." Damon dipped his chin in a sign of respect and then rolled up the window.

The police cruisers, news team, and Damon's SUV trickled out of the clearing and into the woods.

In silence, the busted-up crew stood there watching everyone leave. Candace was cold and numb, shaking from head to toe. Was this what complete shock felt like?

"What about me?" Nox asked.

"What do you mean?" Torren said in an

exhausted voice.

"Well, Damon's out here granting wishes like a damn dragon-genie, you got hearing for your sister, Candace got all her debt paid off, and what am I? Chopped liver?"

Torren's sigh tapered into a frustrated growl.

"Yeah, yeah," Nox muttered, draping his arm over Nevada's shoulder. "I already know what you're going to say." He dropped his voice low and mimicked Torren. "We just lost our alpha and you want to talk about why you didn't get some life-changing gift." Nox snorted and spun him and Nevada to head back toward the house.

"Where are you going?" Torren asked suspiciously.

Nox tossed the *Manners & Shit* book behind him, which landed in the snow near Candace's feet.

"I'm gonna go plan a jailbreak. Even though no one will admit it yet, I'm the MVP of this stupid crew. Our alpha can't rot in shifter prison for a year without his crew. He'll go nuts and burn the world to the ground. Are you coming or not? I'm hungry for pasta and have devious deeds to plan. I need like seven beers. Today sucked balls. Speaking of sucking balls..." Nox's voice became too hard to hear as he and Nevada made their way into the house, leaving Torren and Candace to stare after him dumbly.

Well...okay then.

Devious deeds and jailbreaks.

No one had ever accused them of being the good boys of Damon's Mountains. And now they sure as hell weren't the good boys of Vyr's Mountains.

THIRTEEN

The lobby was full of shifters. The walls and tiles on the floor were the same sterile white, and every air molecule in this room was so saturated with dominance, Candace couldn't breathe. And from the looks on the faces of some of the other inhabitants from Damon's Mountains, they were feeling the heaviness, too.

Two months since Vyr had gone into the shifter prison.

Two months since the crew had been rocked to the core.

Two months since Torren had started doubling his effort to stay stable.

Two months since her mate had begun allowing only one Change a day.

Two months since they'd gone over everything Nox had been able to track down about the shifter prison and realized it was impenetrable.

Two months since they'd had to accept that their alpha had to stay the year.

Two months since Damon Daye had followed through on his promise to pay off her father's debts.

Two months since she'd quit Jem's and gotten a job bagging groceries at Essie's Pantry.

Two months since she and Torren had begun saving money to fix up the sawmill.

Two months that felt like an eternity without Vyr around. Every one of the Sons of Beasts felt the loss. Felt the absence. Felt the hole in the crew. Even Candace's tiger was harder to manage.

Two months since Torren had devoted himself completely to keeping her happy, and also Nox and Nevada, because he was determined to keep the crew together. He was now alpha until Vyr came back home and took the crown again.

Two months, and Damon Daye had paid for the rest of Genevieve's cochlear implant surgery.

This had been the day they'd waited for.

Candace was pacing, her tiger restless around all these unfamiliar shifters.

"Everything is gonna be okay," Torren's father murmured with a kind smile. His leg shook in quick succession as he sat in the chair between his mate, Layla, and Torren. "No one will hurt you here. Everyone knows what you did for Vyr. For Torren, too."

She huffed a laugh and shook her head. "I don't think I'll ever get that day out of my head. Most days I still wish he would've run. I pulled my alpha back to earth and asked the crew to stifle his dragon. I took away his weapons."

"To save him. You did a brave thing for your crew." Kong's chocolate brown eyes were soft and understanding. They were the same color as Torren's now that he had more control over HavoK.

Would Vyr see her betrayal as a good thing, though? She thought not. Every second he spent in that place, she couldn't help but feel it was partly her fault, no matter how much Torren comforted her.

"Come here," Torren murmured, reaching for her from his chair. He hooked a finger in the belt loop of her jeans and tugged her gently toward him.

She gave in and sank onto his lap. They didn't say anything. He just slid his hand up to her neck and gripped the back. He'd learned that was her button. That was what made her feel safe, his firm grip on her, holding her steady. Her cat purred softly, and a slow smile took Torren's lips. He loved having this effect on her. She could tell. He pulled her against his chest and sipped her lips, then rested his forehead onto hers and said, "Today is a good day. One we've looked forward to. You're okay. I'm okay. Nox and Nevada?" he asked, jerking his chin to where they sat cuddled against the wall near them. "They're okay, too. Vyr is gonna be all right. He's stronger than anyone I know, and he's going to come back to us, and we won't ever have to look over our shoulders ever again."

"Swear?" she murmured.

"You trust me?"

She nodded and gripped his wrist to keep his grip on the back of her neck.

"I swear. I'm going to make sure everything is okay."

Strong man. Capable man. He was telling the truth. She could tell from his tone he absolutely believed that he was going to get this crew exactly where it needed to be.

The crowed ramped up their mumbling, and she turned to see a nurse cut through the crowd. She read from a clipboard. "Greyson, the Red Havoc Crew, Kong, Layla, Torren, and Candace. She's ready. Come with me, please."

Candace's heart banged against her chest as they all stood. Greyson was Genevieve's mate and had been sitting silently beside Torren. When the boys stood, Torren gripped his hand and pulled him into a rough hug, hand on the back of his head as he murmured something near Greyson's ear. They both clapped each other on the back and turned to follow the nurse. Torren slid his hand around Candace's and led her past the wall where Nox and Nevada were sitting.

Torren and Candace reached out their hands, and Nox and Nevada squeezed them. Touch had become important lately. It made those strained bonds feel better. They didn't say anything— they were just there. Candace smiled at them and gave a little wave as Torren pulled her toward the hallway behind the others.

The room was a good size, but it was still crowded with Genevieve's mate, crew, and family. She was sitting in a chair against the back wall next to a technician. She wore a red sweater dress and new boots. She and Candace had grown close over text the last couple of months leading up to today, and Genevieve had told her last night she wanted to dress up for her first day of hearing. Candace had matched her and wore a similar dress and boots. Red for Red Havoc. Genevieve waved Torren and Greyson closer, and Candace watched proudly as

Torren knelt beside her, eyes trained on his sister.

The technician signed something to Genevieve who responded with something quick, then nodded.

"She'll hear a beep first," the technician explained to the room.

Everyone went silent, attention on Genevieve, who looked so nervous now. Candace wanted to hug her up and tell her it was all going to be okay, but what if the surgery hadn't worked? Or what if the implant malfunctioned? She understood her nervousness.

Genevieve stared off into space and held up her hand, went tense, and then jerked her gaze to Greyson's who was kneeling right in front of her. He was a big dominant panther shifter, alpha of Red Havoc, and he was kneeling before his mate like Torren often did to Candace.

He squeezed her thighs when he said, "Gen...I love you."

Genevieve clapped her hand over her mouth and tears welled up in her eyes. "I hear you," she said, still a bit thick as if she had cotton in her mouth, but at a soft volume. "I hear you," she repeated, tears streaming down her face. "And I hear me." She cupped Greyson's face. "Again."

"I love you," Greyson said, his voice breaking on the last word.

She slipped her arms around his neck and hugged him so tight, and her shoulders shook with her crying. Suddenly she jerked back and pointed to Torren. "You!"

"Hey, little monkey," Torren said, his voice full of emotion.

"Aaah!" Genevieve cried. "That's me." She signed it as she said it and then laughed as her cheeks turned red.

There wasn't a dry eye in the room as the others spoke to her one by one. Even tough, brawling, dominant Torren sat against the wall and dashed his damp cheek on his shoulder. He blew out a shaky breath as he looked across the room at Candace, his brown eyes full of emotion. And she could feel his relief from here. He'd waited all Genevieve's life for this and had wanted so badly for her to have this moment, and now it was really happening.

People were crowding Genevieve now, talking over each other in excitement, and she was laughing, searching faces in trying to keep up. Torren stood. He made his way out of the crowd to Candace. He pulled her against him and just hugged her like he needed her arms around him. His heart was beating like a bass drum against her cheek.

"I feel like I have everything now," he murmured. "Thank you for getting me here."

"You did the work, Torren."

"Mmm," he rumbled, the sound vibrating from his chest. "You gave me purpose, kept me from breaking. You stood in HavoK's path and asked him for time. You made the man in me stronger, and the silverback in me more patient. Don't downplay your role in my life, Candace. You got me here. I'm damn proud that you're mine."

And in that moment, she knew no matter what, they were going to be okay. No matter what the future held, they could accomplish big things together. She and Torren, Nox and Nevada, and someday Vyr.

Two months ago, she'd fallen into a crew of wild-hearted shifters. A bear, a fox, a gorilla, a tiger…a dragon. She would've never in a million years imagined her life ending up here. But that was the beauty of it—the unknown. How incredible she'd gone to her knees with her dad's death and had to hurt her pride to work a job that made her feel less-than. But what a turnaround when Torren had come into her life.

New job and a crew that, even though completely dysfunctional, loved her. Had her back. Protected her heart. A mate who was the perfect match for her. Someday, Torren's prediction would come true.

Everything was going to be okay.

Better than okay.

She was part of the Sons of Beasts Crew, and they didn't back down, and they didn't quit.

She was friend to Nevada, whom she'd come to adore.

She was new sister to Genevieve, and new

daughter to Kong and Layla.

She was the mate of a man who treated her like his queen.

Two months since her whole life began to turn around for the better because Torren had believed in her worth and showed her she was valuable.

Two months since Torren had accepted every single thing about her and reminded her that even her broken pieces were beautiful.

Two months since she'd joined the crew and changed her stars.

And in another ten months, if they worked hard enough and took care of each other, the Sons of Beasts would be whole again.

EPILOGUE

Torren frowned at the package in the middle of the back-porch table. It was addressed to the *Remainder of the Sons of Beasts Crew* but had no return address.

The handwriting was familiar, but he couldn't place it.

"Here," Nox announced, plopping a plate of bratwursts on the table, "snack time."

Candace giggled clear as a bell beside him and cuddled deeper into the blanket she'd thrown around her shoulders when Torren had called the early-morning crew meeting. She was sitting in her favorite duct-taped pink plastic chair right next to him. "I meant breakfast food or fruit or something," she said.

"Oh, yeah, you're going to have to clarify next time," Nox said, biting into a cooked sausage. Around the giant bite of food, he explained, "I don't get hints, and mind-reading is Vyr's gig."

"I like sausage," Nevada said helpfully as she reached for one.

Nox nodded proudly. "You gonna get stuffed with a ten-inch sausage when we get through this boring-ass meeting and go back to bed."

Nox used to be so annoying, but lately Torren didn't mind him as much. Maybe he was just getting used to him, or maybe he appreciated that the idiot was just about the most loyal person in the whole world and had stepped up as Second in the crew when Vyr had left. This group of friends shouldn't work…but they did. Sure, they fought like cats and dogs most days, and if HavoK didn't fight Nox's grizzly every other day, it was a slow week, but Torren knew from experience that if push came to shove, his mate, Nox, and Nevada would have his back no matter what.

They'd gone and made a family group after all.

Only thing missing? Vyr.

Torren ripped into the package and pulled out a thick book. The cover and spine were a deep burgundy color with a dragon drawn onto the cover with gold filigree. Fancy.

He opened it. Inside, the blank pages had been cut away to make space for a small, handheld video device.

"Whoa," Nox murmured, standing to lock his arms on the table like Torren and look at the book. The brat in his hand was making a grease stain on the old table, but it would just add more character to it, so Torren didn't care. Vyr would probably shit a brick when he saw it, though. That dragon was a neat freak.

Candace cuddled against Torren's side and pushed a small green button that said *play*. God, she smelled good. Shampoo and sleep, and his mate was going to get sausage too, when they were done here. He grinned wickedly just thinking about it. They were trying for a baby now and having a helluva lot of fun practicing.

The blank screen morphed to a scene that stopped Torren's heart. It was a massive room with concrete walls and closed hanger doors along the back. There was a red light flashing over one of them, and the walls were charred and almost black from the scorch marks. There was a bed, no sheets, just a metal frame and a mattress, and on it sat a ghost. At least that's what Torren thought at first.

"Oh, my gosh," Candace whispered as Vyr lifted his shaved head and stared directly into the camera. One of his eyes was human blue, but one was the silver of his dragon. Fuck. He looked exhausted, pale, and his fists were clenched on his knees like he was pissed.

"I said I don't want to do interviews," he growled in a voice that echoed around the room with power.

"Your father has requested this," a woman's voice sounded from behind the camera.

Vyr's hands clenched even tighter, and his face

twisted in rage.

"What are your feelings after being here for six months?"

"I don't have feelings. Never did."

There was a scribbling noise as the interviewer jotted down notes. "I've read your file and am aware you have had some issues with authority. What can this facility do to make this experience easier on you?"

"You mean what can they do to control me better?"

"Sure."

Vyr ripped his gaze away from her and didn't answer.

She tried again. "If you could have one thing here, for comfort, what would it be?"

His voice cracked on the answer. "My crew."

Those two words gutted Torren. Vyr looked like shit, like he'd been going through literal hell, and he was admitting he needed them. He'd never admitted to needing anyone. This was really bad.

The interviewer's voice dropped to a barely

audible whisper. "They're trying to take your dragon. If you want to say something, request something, ask for help...do it now."

When Vyr slid his half-human, half-dragon gaze to the woman, his mask of rage had fallen. He swallowed hard and said, "Breaking and entering."

"What?"

"Vandalism. Illegal fights."

Vyr blinked slowly and locked that fiery gaze on the camera. There was power in his voice as he ordered, "Come. Here."

The camera clicked to black.

"Holy shit," Nox murmured.

"What does this mean?" Nevada asked in a small, scared voice.

The handwriting on the address suddenly clicked into place. It belonged to Damon Daye. He'd helped put Vyr in that awful place, and now he was trying to help his son? Torren needed to figure out what Damon's end game was before they did this, for the protection of his crew.

Candace was staring up at Torren with a grim

set to her mouth, as if she already knew where he was going to go with this.

"Seriously, what did he mean?" Nevada asked louder.

Torren pulled Candace tighter against his ribs and sighed. "He just listed things that would get us minimal time in shifter prison."

"Meaning?" Candace asked, but her voice was full of steel like she already knew. She already looked on board with this.

"Meaning, we can't break into that facility and get him out. But our alpha just ordered us to come save his dragon."

"We're getting arrested?" Nox asked a little too excitedly. "I'm in!"

Nevada looked nervous as hell, but she lifted two fingers in the air. "It's Vyr. He looks bad. He's ours. I'm in."

Candace gently clenched her teeth onto Torren's bicep. She eased back and then shook her head at him with a small grin on her lips. "Well, if we're goin' to Hell, we might as well do it thoroughly.

I'm in."

"Yeaaah!" Nox crowed. "Let's go fuck some shit up! I've got, like, thirty ideas already. We need to find a swan-sitter for Mr. Diddles."

Torren chuckled and roughly ran his hands through his hair. God, they couldn't just be well-behaved for any amount of time before they found trouble.

But then again? That's what they'd signed up for the day they made this crew. This was the motherfuckin' Z-Team. Total screw-ups and proud. They weren't built to be a quiet crew.

"All right," Torren murmured, allowing a slow, wicked smile as he looked around at his people, his friends, his family group…his mate. "Let's go save the Red Dragon."

Want more of these characters?

Son of Kong is the second book in the Sons of Beasts series.

For more of these characters, check out these other books from T. S. Joyce.

Son of the Cursed Bear
(Sons of Beasts, Book 1)

Son of the Dragon
(Sons of Beasts, Book 3)

This is a spinoff series set in the Damon's Mountains universe. Start with Lumberjack Werebear to enjoy the very beginning of this adventure.

About the Author

T.S. Joyce is devoted to bringing hot shifter romances to readers. Hungry alpha males are her calling card, and the wilder the men, the more she'll make them pour their hearts out. She werebear swears there'll be no swooning heroines in her books. It takes tough-as-nails women to handle her shifters.

She lives in a tiny town, outside of a tiny city, and devotes her life to writing big stories. Foodie, wolf whisperer, ninja, thief of tiny bottles of awesome smelling hotel shampoo, nap connoisseur, movie fanatic, and zombie slayer, and most of this bio is true.

Bear Shifters? Check

Smoldering Alpha Hotness? Double Check

Sexy Scenes? Fasten up your girdles, ladies and gents, it's gonna to be a wild ride.

> For more information on T. S. Joyce's work,
> visit her website at
> www.tsjoyce.com

Made in the USA
Coppell, TX
26 August 2023